Cynosura

by

Tito Perdue

Books by Tito Perdue

Lee (1991)
The New Austerities (1994)
Opportunities in Alabama Agriculture (1994)
The Sweet-Scented Manuscript (2004)
Fields of Asphodel (2007)
The Node (2011)
Morning Crafts (2013)
Reuben (2014)
The Builder: William's House I (2016)
The Churl: William's House II (2016)
The Engineer: William's House III (2016)
The Bachelor: William's House IV (2016)

Cynosura

by

Tito Perdue

Standard American Publishing Company-
Brent, Alabama
2020

This book is dedicated to its subject, to that certain kind of woman who knows why she exists. How rare such people be! I personally have heard of women who imagine that they dropped to earth in order more or less to do what men are designed to do.

The more dispositively *unlike* are men and women, the more electrifying their encounters. Spartan soldiers, it is reported, were only seldom allowed to visit their own wives. Try to imagine the quality of those interviews, strangers from outer space hungry for each other.

Would like to have been there.

One

As you consider these first pages (assuming that you will), try to understand that the information came to me secondhand. Even so, I am confident that I have rendered the dialogue at least as accurately as the original speakers, if not indeed more so. My sources were consistent, however, and I am perfectly confident of the truthfulness of this account, which I now offer to those willing to receive it.

Two

Born under the sign of Saturn, he came forth on a dark and rainy night in that part of Tennessee whence a person can distantly see the gorgeous mountain range that distinguishes that exceptional state. Dark and rainy night? We have no proof of that or even that the boy had aught to do with Saturn or any other such matter. He did come forth, however, and in Tennessee, and we know the date within a few months of the actual event.

Nothing could have been better than the small-town South in those days, nothing more propitious for the intellection that he was to exemplify later on. By the age of nine, he had already had three girlfriends, had visited the Gulf Coast, and had caught his full meed of flounder and speckled trout. He played baseball, a failed effort that brought him to football in which he proved uniquely willing to bring down, or try so to do, even the most intimidating of ball carriers. It is remarkable that at so young an age, he had determined that it were better to die immediately than fail to make the best efforts available to him. It yielded him a broken nose (broken three times) and a boxer's profile that kept any possibility of handsomeness completely out of reach.

His father was not especially handsome either, and in fact really had been a boxer in his college days. They used to spar with each other in comradely fashion, until the child turned fifteen. You will look in vain for any aspersions against those parents of his. They lived and died, as did the girl shortly to be described, before the full onset of the postmodern age. In any event, we wouldn't have known it even if his parents had been the worst in the world. But they were not. As between the worst and best, they ranked much nearer the last-mentioned.

He was given a series of ever-larger dogs as his own size also grew larger. Desperately in love with each of them, yet he never taught a single one even the barest minimum of English speech. By twelve he played the trombone, but had to wait till fourteen before his instructor took him off to one side and described in depth how the boy had no talent whatsoever. Having failed at that, he jumped into stamp collecting.

More than dogs, he adored girls, especially those with oval faces that held so many lips and eyes and so many unpredictable expressions. He had seen how these creatures could produce the most realistic-looking smiles even when they didn't feel like it, an enormous problem for parents, teachers, and males in general. With more stamps than girls, he had kissed only one of them (girls, not stamps) before 1949. Other of his misbehaviors included the theft of a wallet, a yo-yo, and a good number of fishing lures from a downtown store managed by a middle-age woman of unusual naïveté. Some of that merchandise—and this is perhaps the most implausible part of the story—he was said to have returned.

In September 1950, he left home and ventured into the ten-acre woods that bordered the neighborhood on that side. There an abandoned three-storey schoolhouse extended above the treetops, a brick structure that two generations earlier had served the town's white youths of high-school age. No one went there anymore, save only occasionally a hobo seeking shelter or neighborhood children using the place as a fort. Never was he to forget it, that fading inscription still to be seen on one of the blackboards, a piece of information about the War of 1812 written by an earnest teacher now rotting in the grave. He could imagine the tumult that once had filled these halls, the pushing and shoving and the love affairs that had endured for perhaps a month or so before dwindling down to nothing save a few faint, random memories fading away in ageing brains. How strange all things were! When a person dies, that person is either dead, or else he goes on to some other tenure somewhere else. In the first instance, a man ought to do what he can in his brief time. In the second, he may hope to be welcomed by cheering crowds.

These were heavy thoughts for a twelve-year-old, but bringing into play his general indifference to anything relating to his own far-away death, he walked to the edge of the roof of that multi-storey structure, a half-acre expanse littered with tree branches and pine cones, two exhausted whiskey bottles, and a dozen dead birds, an excellent platform whence he could survey that fraction of the city that mattered to him. His own home he saw, and his morose father stooped over in the yard severing crabgrass roots with his pocket knife. A pipe hung from his mouth, and his glasses sat slightly askew his largish nose, a genealogical feature that also afflicted the boy on the roof. He could identify the home of Glenda Blight, but any hope that she would come to him someday, saying, "I love you *so much*, I really do," any such hope as that had long ago withered away in the darkness of his bedroom.

Just then he noticed a kite flying over the golf course three blocks away, a bright blue one with a human face on it. From somewhere a half-dozen dogs were barking at some cause too inconsequential to hold their attention for very long, while nearer he could hear the resonating voice of a well-known reporter addressing himself by radio to America and ships at sea. News about Korea, the boy had to suppose. His mind turned then to the map of that region and some of the stamps in his two-volume collection. He was thinking too rapidly now and about too many different subjects all at once. In the fullness of time, this was the peculiarity that would finally ruin him.

Three

If you've come this far in my account, I hope you'll not turn back now. He said he used to run home from school to listen to his radio and to those voices that came from so far away. But mostly they came from New York City where the speakers, as he pictured them, were well-dressed men and women standing around a microphone. Afterwards they would retire to a favorite nightclub and drink drinks while listening to a beautiful singer—such was his knowledge of New York City and its things.

Those were the days. But the best was yet to come, coming when his father, tired from a hard day's work, entered through the back door with some little gift in his jacket pocket. He was a wistful man, that one, somewhat older in appearance than he should have been. He would go quickly through his newspaper and then give a few minutes to the radio, skeptical of most of what he heard. Half an hour later—it never failed— the man was sleeping and the ash on his cigarette was threatening to fall into his lap. And did sometimes fall, whereupon the man would come to his feet and brush the sparks from his trouser pants.

His father had possibly four suits in total, but they all looked just alike. His pockets flared out, filled to the limit with a cigarette lighter, a half-pound of silver change, an engineer's eraser, a pocket knife, and a hazelnut of peculiar shape.

And all this time the boy's mother had been working in the kitchen. She might serve them boiled chicken with dumplings and gravy, cornbread and buttermilk, okra, biscuits with butter and jam, etcetera, the result of her hours at the stove and sink. At first she wore an apron with a picture of a cow on it, and in later years a cartoon character dressed in a yellow hat.

The boy would then waste a few minutes with his homework, simpleminded stuff that he could finish within minutes while getting it perfect. Of course his parents had to admonish him from time to time, but had trouble finding cause. He had friends, girlfriends even, and was remarkably good at football, despite being so untowardly small for his size. For the other part, what secret evils did the child harbor in his tetrahedral head? These are to be described at greater length later on.

Four

Obviously this is to be a focused account, made so in the hope that those with narrow attention spans will remain "on board," as it were. Not that I could do otherwise with my limited information.

The boy must have possessed a thousand stamps by now, selecting them as if for an art gallery. Want the key to his life? Beauty, beauty, beauty, conduits, he was eventually to say, to life on higher planes. Eruptions in the fabric of life that offer a view of the ineffable. Or offers it anyway to those who earn it.

He so loved the night, he would wallow in it, postponing for as long as he could the onset of sleep. His room permitted the introduction of light beams from the outside traffic, a source of problematic shadows seen by him as men slaughtering each other with knives, or cats and dogs, or lightning sticks, or naked women with good physiques.

Five

He grew and developed and sometimes took a step sideways or in the wrong direction. Lest he be accused of cheating, he began making deliberate errors on his tests and homework. He hadn't reached the stage, not yet, of acknowledging his superiority, far less of letting it be seen. He was still able to have friends, therefore, and to land himself in trouble along with the best of them. He never lost a fight and therefore didn't need to have many.

As reported, he wasn't especially handsome, not yet nor ever, and could pass through a crowd without accumulating the sort of female attention he wanted. He could, however, venture downtown whenever he wanted; it was 1950 in the South, and half the people he encountered were long-term friends of his. Movies were eleven cents, no matter how long he remained in his seat. *And* he could stroll home alone in the dark provided he arrived no later than ten o'clock. Those were the days.

All this nostalgia says nothing, however, about his growing bitterness, namely that life was not nearly as good as it should have been. Throughout his whole life, *it was always the present moment that was bad*, never mind what the rest was like. He had seen films and read books in which life was at full force *all the time*, in the days of Achilles for example, or Robin Hood and the others. There was something wrong with a world that wouldn't allow these sorts of experiences to attend him *always*, forever, permanently without end. He craved to be put to sea in an ocean of everlasting bliss, beauty, and heroism, adored uselessly by millions of girls. Knowing he would never have it, or not all of it anyway, he grew morose and turned away from his one-time friends.

"You think you're better than everybody else. Don't you?"

He nodded sadly.

He remained so small that by the age of thirteen, he was still able to get into the movies for eleven cents. His grades were perfect save only in demeanor, which he despised. He had taken an interest in mathematics, but only by dint of hard effort was he able to do well in it. Neither in music nor in mathematics did he boast any special talent, though he respected both of them from a certain distance. His *real* destiny was scheduled for elsewhere, in necromancy perhaps, or, as he was beginning to believe, within one of the new parallel universes coming all too slowly into focus in the country's best heads.

He was growing up meantime, and by age of fourteen was just ten or fifteen percent smaller than his colleagues. Even now, he had never lost a fight. He had a chemistry set and sixteen model airplanes hanging by threads from his bedroom ceiling. Had a dog and a great many East European postage stamps. Could swim a mile without stopping. He had become an Eagle Scout and had gone on camp-outs unaccompanied by others. He detested all things that interfered with his radio programs.

Enough of this, you have the general idea.

Six

Adolescence came down on him like a crowd of Assyrians clad in purple and gold. He woke up tumescent and went to sleep that way. His mental facilities were likewise extended, and he had hardly entered the 1950s before he had become one of the library's most pestilential visitors.

"You again! So what's it going to be *this* time?" She did smile, however. (It was here, he believed, that he first learned to make himself acceptable to older women.) Normally he would proceed to the rear of the building where the little bit of light bestowed a mysterious quality on the books themselves. He preferred fat books with dark blue bindings, assumed by him to be especially profound. At first, he confined himself to fiction and had a high opinion of everything he read. It awed him that anyone could write so many words in just one lifetime. But primarily it was the people portrayed in those books, serious individuals with thoughts and emotions that he had thought were his alone. Whatever his own mind invented, it had already occurred to his favorite authors, problematic men a great deal like himself. His silence increased and his face took on a hooded expression.

His eighth-grade class did have a smattering of girls in it, but only two were beautiful. And yet he was also polite to the others. *More* polite, in fact.

Seven

Next to be considered is the girl referenced in the title. Some people are born to be exceptional and, urged by Time, become continually more so. Thinking back on it, she was to remember the thunder and lightning and the patter on the wall of the branches that around the thatch eves ran. A conjunction of misperceptions had, however, led her to believe that her two different parents were one and the same. And: "Must I indeed be an only child," she wondered, "or are others on the way?"

Later she began to have experiences of music on the radio, trucks moving down the highway, the yard crowded with red chickens, and not much else.

Years went by, three of them to be roughly precise. Began now her twenty-two-year assignment of beauty and nose-grinding work. Already she was pretty and already smart. Nothing worried her parents more.

Eight

Truth was, she craved to be a bird. Often in those days she could have been seen standing out in the Sun, eight years old, her milk-colored hair already fetching comments from the townspeople. She could write on paper, do mathematics all the way to long division, silent as a caterpillar as she later described herself to me. It was yet another truth that she wanted to be done with childhood and to fulfill her earthly assignment as soon as possible. Of course, I didn't know what to make of such talk at that time.

Unhappily for happiness, she had two sisters and a brother, one of them technically an imbecile and the others so ordinary they could have dissolved away forever in any good-sized crowd. The eldest of the lot, our *Cynosura* (I call her), had overall charge of these people whenever their mother was busy in the cafeteria of the downtown tractor parts manufacturer, or when cleaning someone's house, or minding someone's children. All their lives, this mother and her husband were to give more to the nation than ever the nation even thought about giving back to them, the essential pre-condition of the American system. Already she saw, their precocious child, that it was money that com-manded effort instead of the other way around. Four-teen years later it was I myself who said: "We reward people in accord with their economic value. Better we rewarded them in accord with their value."

And she who said: "People like that don't need much reward."

You can imagine her in those days, sitting on the front porch with an idiot in her lap. Childish and naïve, Christianized, democratized, equalized, she believed it right to defray her own abilities — and she knew by now that she had some — defray them in an unavailing effort to lift her brother to just the most basic level. She wiped away his snot, using for that purpose her ironed and laundered kerchief. She whispered stories into those dead, dumb ears while standing at the stove. Her eyes were as diamonds, *his* were lumps of coal.

Nine

Apart from a general passivity and capitulationist mindset, there was nothing about the girl's father that needs criticizing. An uneducated person, ignorant of the new technology, society had no better use for the old man than to put him atop a grain elevator to weigh the corn and soybeans brought to him by the nearby growers. From this post, he could see the medieval Tennessee countryside with its barns and cattle, its large and small cities apportioned in higgledy-piggledy fashion across the wrinkled countryside. His money was small, and any residual ambitions of his had long before this been set off to one side. He had a shotgun, a dog, a truck, and a television, and had been permitted to enjoy in silence the genial indifference accorded him by the more active citizens. He did have that daughter. He used to sit at table, glancing in her direction from time to time. How on Earth had she arrived on this planet? Her advice was better than her mother's, her figure was precocious, and though she carried sunshine in her hair, yet her face had somewhat of a melancholy cast. This happens sometimes, a certain assemblage of female material brought together in paradise by dwarves working in unsleeping shifts. Not to mention an IQ assayed variously at one hundred twenty-seven and one hundred thirty-two.

The mother of this miracle was a drab sort of individual consecrated mostly to slopping the hogs, peering into the oven, and bending over the ironing board. Life, she thought, was what she saw around her. Very seldom did she chide her eldest daughter, or anyway not until that day she espied her in the shower. Not for a long time had she seen the girl in her naked condition.

"Oh, my lands," she said, "you're going to get in trouble looking like that!"

"I want to."

"There's no call for that, baby! You be careful now, I mean it."

It is of course true that the country's prettiest girls always derive from the southeastern countryside. All that cornbread and black-eyed peas, those large-eye animals protected by barbwire fences. Look at her now and think of her riding on a cow. She did that.

By 1954, the town began to be aware of her. Cars slowed, and boys anguished at the sight of her. What, did she think she was a goddamn *queen* or something? Kill her. As for the women, it was too late now to prevent her from having come to Earth those fourteen years ago. Only a bath of hot acid could now suffice.

Her father curtained the windows. These days she

was permitted to wander but to the edge of the property, a limitation that seemed not to bother her. She had her horse and pigs, and more recently her rented violin. Her nose was alert, her forehead luminous, while her agile breasts had been chosen from the world's very best. Wickedly, she preferred tight sweaters.

Ten

She wasted years trying to become as modest and friendly and shallow as America insists. Wasted years on her idiot brother who grew ever more stupid the more she lavished on him. Squandered years practicing tolerance and learning how to smile. She tried so hard to be average and win friends to her side. Her shoes were well-kept and small enough to fit her. She had a green beret, the gift of a teacher. She dasn't wear it, however, lest she violate beauty's limits.

From small beginnings, her cosmetics trove soon filled both drawers, and by 1954 it needed most of her wee salary to sustain it. Obviously she had given up on hiding her . . . aplomb. On the contrary, she learned the joys of sticking it in people's faces. Better still was the joy of being hated.

Her brother was at last consigned to the state asylum while her two sisters remained at freedom to pursue their low-level ways. The youngest of them had a baby, also perhaps an idiot, who was to need eight years to learn to crawl. The remaining sister, the better of the two, studied social work and married a soldier stationed in Germany. Free now of the burden these people had imposed and lucky enough to have a docile mother, the Divine One went about her project of getting perfect grades while earning $2.25 per hour as a part-time bookkeeper at the nearby Ford distributorship, this in addition to managing the family farm. She proved good at buying cattle and disposing of them at profitable prices. She understood the sort of people who adhere to home and soil, and never in her whole twenty-two-year-long life was she ever to impugn them in any way whatsoever. She respected animals, too, particularly on account of their patience and willingness to submit to higher intelligences. Admired their ability to endure the weather and consume foodstuffs that she preferred to avoid. She watched them copulating in the field, an ambiguous experience. Ignorant of history, these barnyard creatures believed their own generation to be the first of its kind. They replied to their surroundings, but not a single one of them knew that he or she actually existed. Each night was a new terrifying experience. Her own brother had known better than that.

It was Thursday, 1955, that I encountered this angel (angel in a green sweater) for the first time. I had come to town on some mission or another—I forget why—when she was pointed out to me, a figment from another planet. "Gracious!" said I. (I'm a genteel type, and at that time was employed as Associate Professor of Chemistry at the University of Tennessee.) "Gracious! What is *that*?"

She floated past, her sweater just a bit too tight, her face calm, and her head tilted slightly skyward. I was given a two-second glimpse of her profile, a golden coin of Syracuse. Already she knew all things, good and bad, and unlike the boy described below and above, accepted everything in full serenity. See how much a Professor can divine in just two seconds flat?

She was still living at home, still supervising the cows, still dithering with her violin. And then on Wednesday came the second-best day of her career when she was made to surrender her violin and take up the cello instead, a profounder and more mellow instrument withal. It sorted perfectly with her gorgeous face and those traces of far-away melancholy in her eyes.

Eleven

And then at age seventeen she went off to college, a blessing that came to her in the form of a scholarship. She had been seen playing on her enormous guitar [*sic*] while dressed in a gown that failed to obscure her figure. It was required dress for girls in the orchestra, a boon for girls like this one. Seen, I started to say, by an alumnus of the University who happened also to be a significant donor to that school. She had just given a performance of Kodály's unaccompanied cello sonata, her own fourth-favorite piece, and he came upon her just as she was exiting the auditorium. Her father had taken charge of the instrument and was transporting it back to the truck in a bespoken cardboard "suitcase" that conformed to the size of the thing. Early April in Tennessee it was, and the weather was sweet.

"No, you're very good," the alumnus said. "Have you been playing long?"

"Near 'bout a year," her father replied. "But we didn't try to stop her."

"Do you have a coach?"

"Mr. Osborn," the girl's father again replied. "Track and field, don't you know. But we put a stop to it. Not good for girls."

They were by now in the outside world with the departing audience, some hundred or more of them giving wide berth to the celestial-looking cellist. Her hair was done up in the way that she was to insist upon in the following years.

"They make her dress like that."

"When do you graduate?"

"Fifty-two days. Not me, her."

Together the man and daughter lifted the instrument into the back of the truck and were quite prepared, it seemed, to abandon the alien where he stood.

"Well, g'night I reckon."

"Have you thought of college?"

The vehicle actually did go forward a few inches.

"Say what?"

"College. How are your grades?"

"Nothing wrong with those grades! Just about the best anywhere around here, I reckon."

"Is that right?" the stranger asked, coming near and inserting his face to within about six inches of the one belonging to the girl. "How good, exactly?"

She turned and looked at him calmly.

"Perfect. Except for attendance."

"Perfect?"

"That's what she said."

They drove to the farm, stopping along the way for a can of tomato paste and a half-gallon of milk. It was not an impressive building, the family's, and some work was needed on the roof. A hoofed animal of some nature waited on the porch, and the girl's mother was at the ironing board.

It was past nine o'clock already, wherefore they were given but a slice of warmed-over blackberry pie with a wedge of cheese on top. All four optioned for coffee as well. Very soon the girl dispersed to her own room to change into other clothes, a decision the stranger regretted. He didn't call her back, however. That left just three of them to discuss the weather and associated topics.

"Really, she ought to attend college, that girl of yours."

"I know it. But it's not as easy as what you people seem to think. She's got a job now, and there's her mother and me."

"You're both in bad health, then?"

"We will be. And the *herd*. I can't do everything."

"No, no one wants that. What would it cost to hire someone, I wonder?"

"Plenty, that's what. Real plenty."

"She's got talent, I think."

"Yeah, we figured that out long time ago. And Sarah, too, she's real good at making clothes and so on. All my babies are good. Except one."

"And he can't help it," the mother added quickly.

"I do believe I could get that girl—what's her name?—could get her into a good college," the strange man said. "And I know just the one, too."

The man and wife gazed at each other.

"Imagine that. Coledge."

She practiced every day while holding down a full-time job, and by autumn had accumulated money enough and sufficient virtuosity to enter music school with better than two thousand dollars' worth of money, cash, and clothes. Conservative with mascara and eye liner, she gave preference to low heels, blue-plaid skirts (rather short ones, actually), and white sweaters that failed to deemphasize her cultured breasts. Her demeanor was conservative, forbidding even, while her face remained forever serene. She was thinking rapidly but calmly, her eyes fixed upon a place in the clouds. No one called to her, or anyway not from a remove of less than about forty feet. From that distance she might hear someone cooing lewdly in her direction, negro voices that didn't register on her. Her cello was well-formed, but no one ever confused it for the girl herself.

She entered the departmental building on that first Friday and found her way to the Chairman's office, a bald man, not unfriendly, who looked her over with some concern before signaling her to a chair. She sat and waited patiently, her knees, in good hosiery, extending perhaps three inches beyond her hem. The man glanced in that direction.

"So. Cello?"

"Yes. And harp."

"Really? We can use *that*."

She took out a cigarette and lit it with a red-headed kitchen match of about two inches in length. It produced a considerable flame that loitered briefly in mid-air. With her phosphorescent hair, lipstick, knees, and the slim leather briefcase that held her music, she comprised a much-better-than-ordinary scene.

"And you're the one who . . ." (He rifled through his papers) ". . . was given the Woodridge Fellowship?"

"Yes."

"Good for you. It even covers your books, I believe."

No reply. She wasn't responsible for what he believed. It also covered her living expenses up to three thousand two hundred dollars for the nine-month session.

"You'll have to work very hard to hold on to that." (Now, though he really didn't want to, he glanced at her knees.) "Lots of applicants. New ones every year."

There was a secretary in the next office, a prune-like manifestation staring at the knees through the open door.

"Will you be using the dormitory?"

No, she had taken a two-room apartment on the west side of college, an airy dwelling, she was told, at fifty-two dollars per month. Having finished with the chairman, she now hurried across campus to her new place, never entirely unaware of those who stared at her wherever she went.

It was a stern-looking woman who opened for her. After a brief discussion, and after seeming to approve of the girl's . . . aplomb, the woman softened somewhat. She conducted the girl up two flights and into the expensive (expensive for that time) two-room affair with its desk and chair, its leather sofa and, in the next room, its narrow but amenable-looking bed that along with its pillow and coverings resembled a dumpling. The quilt was pink and blue and had been constructed, she divined, by three gossiping women sharing one eye between them. The window, otherwise broad enough to allow a person to pass through it, had been fitted with bars. She rented the place at once.

"I actually prefer music students," the landlady revealed. "Though not so much the trumpet players, of course."

They smiled at each other.

"I go to nearly all the concerts. And every one of the operas without fail. But you, you look like a stringed instrument to me."

"Cello," the girl confessed. "And harp, when it's needed."

"Oh, good gracious yes, I do like the harp. We're going to get along real fine."

She was left alone, the girl, in her appealing apartment. There remained now but to retrace the three-quarter-mile hike back to campus to gather her instrument—two cars, both driven by charitable young men, offered to drive her—and then to toddle on back to her first private quarters. To explore the rooms in full required better than an hour.

Twelve

By this time, a certain amount of time had gone by. They hadn't yet realized, his parents had not, that he had already broken with them, but had carried it out so gently that they weren't aware of it.

"It surprises me," the old man said, "that you haven't been more active. Student government and so forth. Sports. No, that could be good for your career. Wish I'd done that."

The boy nodded. "Right. I'm pretty good at tennis, though."

"Yes, you are! Good."

And in short, the man wanted what was most advantageous for the boy within the context of the unanimity of the day. Instead, the miscreant continued to read unnecessarily heavy books in blue covers organized by size in his personal cabinet. Gleaning for wisdom (as he represented himself to me), he had been grappling with Nietzsche, Spengler, Evola, and other heavyweight authors whom he only halfway understood. Meantime his tennis remained at high levels, and in order to stay in good physical condition he had added chess to his inventory of self-inflicted things.

Chess: he must have wasted five hundred hours on this minuscule pursuit before it finally dawned on him that he was *not* becoming a more excellent or more dangerous person as a result, and in place of that began to read up on female psychology and how to bring some of those people into his orbit. He loved no one, but wanted very much to be loved by beautiful girls. Unusual for a boy of his age, he thought of sex as but a trivial pursuit as compared to being *desired*, hopelessly desired by girls pursuant to abandoning them, a peculiarity of his that some have seen as just short of outright mental illness. He began to groom himself, pleased that it set him off from his colleagues. There is no doubt that he would have been made to pay for his vanity had he not in the meanwhile become friendly with a former professional boxer, an alcoholic willing for a liter of beer to spend an hour or two per week with him.

"Speed," the man had said, "*that's* the ticket. And don't be trying to hit a man in the goddamn head, that won't do any good. Hit *through* the head and out the other side. You fuck up his brains, he won't hit back. Good! Do it again."

He studied hard, the boy, studying also the "integrity," as he thought of it, the integrity inscribed on that man's face in terms of his bent nose and what looked like boils.

There is among the males of the world an international communication system that tells whether or not another male may be set upon with a decent possibility of success. To activate the system needs only a single event, in this case when the boy had just completed his sixteenth year and dared to wear a suit and tie to algebra class. Remember, he weighed hardly one hundred thirty pounds at that juncture but did have good speed, pretty good, and had trained himself to concentrate on uppercuts to places where bone breakage was most available.

Paisley was his favorite color, and dark blue the pattern he chiefly preferred. He kept his socks in good order, too, and by the end of his junior year had an academic record that was the most nearly perfect in the whole organization. To be sure, he was inordinately ambitious, though not precisely in the way the adult world approved. Just sixteen years old, he was already a little bit "dangerous," and after his first and only fight, the son-of-a-bitch felt he was *on his way*.

Thirteen

By the middle 1950s, he had read so much and had so often heard that history follows a cyclical path that he had begun seriously to doubt it. Finally on Thursday, he put together a paper for his teacher wherein he maintained that history is rather like a kaleidoscope in which elements come together at hazard to form unique tableaux that never repeat. He read the report twice, did his teacher, and then gave it back with compliments. It was clear he had understood none of it. But even that was better than the editors of scholarly journals who never replied at all.

By this time, he was working fifteen hours per week at a used-furniture store where the customers were few and far between. This was the time he read Spengler's famous work, a distracting project that caused him to lose his job. In this effort, he had had to read lines of text when what he really wanted was to pour the stuff in through his ear.

His next position required him to stand at a food counter and put the people's purchases, female customers mostly, put them, the purchases not the purchasers, in brown paper bags. He might often be asked to carry the stuff out to the woman's car, a likeable duty if the woman was less than forty. He has admitted to me that he would try to follow several paces behind so as to watch their hips yawing back and forth. It wasn't the first time the boy's confessions made me worry about him. And yet he seemed like a reasonable person, groomed and bathed and not bad-looking, his expression made unnaturally pleasant by force of will. Three days of this and his tips were larger than his wages.

Wage: his earnings were small, becoming smaller after certain subtractions relating to a number of things.

And yet he never went so far as actually to steal from the store, never mind how much that was urged by his fellow workers. His policy was never to get into conflict with policemen working on the bounty system. Already he had learned this much, that anyone stealing less than a million dollars at a time could get into serious trouble indeed.

He was a fortunate young person, as he believed. No one troubled him save when one or another of his parents wanted only the best for him. He had his own room in the southwest corner of the house, a narrow cell that however gave him the space he needed for his desk and globe, his reference books, a cheap telescope that let him see into peoples' homes, and a large black typewriter bought for almost nothing at a pawn shop run by an East European of some kind. The man's beard was immense and held more termites than the rotting structure chosen for his business. As a person of that kind, he had brought together all manner of odds and ends, especially the former. Our hero used to loiter there at regular intervals, entranced by the rubbish on display. There was a glass cabinet (locked) holding a golden watch or two, a switchblade knife with an engraving on the blade, and a second-hand .32-caliber revolver appropriate for a woman's purse. Next to the implement itself, six cartridges stood at full height. Dangerous weapons, but not half so dangerous as his increasing education and smart grooming. They looked at each other, the shopkeeper and he.

He studied chemistry but had to resort to the library for a more thoroughgoing text. Intrigued by the atomic schemata and the resemblance between the elements and certain personality types, he looked to the time when thousand-proton atoms might be synthesized. He was optimistic, if not about the world, about science, at any rate. Enough science and the world might become a better place, offering experiences as good as certain moments in certain music pieces.

Wednesday morning, he was called to the Principal's office and shown to a chair that allowed the two of them to look at one another. Warned in advance, the boy was wearing a tie with a decent pattern on it and his shoes were black.

"I keep hearing about you," the man said, smiling. "Another perfect record. And not the first time, either!"

The child pretended to look as if he were surprised, even embarrassed, at such good news. He blushed, or tried to, and looked down at his black shoes. He knew of course that his personal development came in spates, sometimes even falling off to garden-variety levels.

"Have you thought of college?"

"Sir? Well, I'd like to. But, you know, I've already been too much of a burden on my parents."

"Oh, I don't think that's true. You earn your own money, is what I hear."

He couldn't deny it. Behind him, the man possessed some of the reference materials the boy held in his own narrow room—a statistical survey of the economies and resources of the world's countries, an atlas, phone directory, and a formulary with the picture on the jacket of a molecule the boy wasn't immediately able to identify.

"Well, you certainly must go to college K----------." (He used the boy's name.) "A huge shame not to. Huge. What do you think?"

"Sir? Well, I need to give that some thought." And then, brightly: "My uncle went to college."

"See what I mean? You go, too. Promise?"

The boy nodded thoughtfully.

He strode home through scads of girls and after

changing shirts and leaving his books behind, loped over to his working place where right away he went to his duties with a smile. He could not say that he had a good opinion of the foodstuffs these people were buying, nor of their behavior. In short, they were slobs. He saw a fat man in shorts, his legs full of varicose veins. Slobs. And yet these were the sovereign rulers of this rich and powerful country that at one time had found inspiration from the Greeks.

Something now began to happen; more and more often he could hear no sounds from anywhere. He lived "inside his brain," he once said, and no longer allowed "exoteric" things to impinge on it. Calm, deaf, he lifted the women's purchases one by one and put them away in good order in the brown paper sack designed to contain them. At one time, the getting of food was humanity's most fraught requirement; today it could be done by persons who didn't even know where food came from. Was that bad? No, he said, not if it fitted people for higher endeavors than grubbing in the soil.

He was perhaps the most prematurely serious seventeen-year-old on record. How it was that other young people could spend so much time laughing and smiling and jumping up and down was for him one of the most puzzling of things. One could have a lot more fun by being serious. Bending down to earth and studying at close range the little creatures in the dirt whilst planting gardenias on behalf of his mother—that for him gave much more pleasure than any possible cans of beer. He tended therefore to keep largely to himself while at the same time always trying to assuage his parents' fears.

"No, no," he might say. "I *like* what I do."

"Yes, of course, but . . ."

"Like girls, too, and . . ."

"Too much."

". . . and if I wanted friends, I could have as many as I want."

"But . . ."

"And I'll have a good career, too. Just you wait and see."

They suffered for him, right up until late winter when they gave up the struggle and let him take a room that was nearer both to school and to his place of work. He had saved nearly five hundred dollars since September, and with the single sole exception of a former friend of his (now lodged in the county jail), he was the only high school student with his own dwelling place. His prestige increased. And then to put the seal on it, he bought for himself an eight-cylinder car with less than one hundred thousand miles on it.

He had chosen a room that was as long and as narrow, almost, as the one he had used at home. Supplied with a bed (also long and narrow), he added a used desk with cigarette burns on it, a fully usable appliance costing just five dollars. He immediately searched the drawer of course, finding only dust and a chit of paper with something written on it. He then added two hundred sheets of typing paper to the space and hid several large bills of currency in the pile. Other money he kept with him at all times, twenty or thirty dollars where he could get at it quickly. He did not yet carry the .32-caliber revolver acquired at small price from his second-favorite downtown pawn shop. He was a dark-headed boy, precocious and unfriendly. No matter the project, he expected to do better than anyone else. From a distance, he offered a stubborn-looking figure, moving step by step to where he wished to go.

His cultural tastes were immature of course, and until he began to acquaint himself with some of the recordings in his father's fine collection, he continued to accept much of the music of his generation. He would often borrow two or three of these discs on his visits.

His grades continued good, even if not quite so good as before he had taken it upon himself to earn his own money. He knew of course that in case of need, his family would still support him, quite a different situation than actual poverty. Came December, he was promoted and now, instead of standing at the counter in an apron and smile, he passed the time in the back room doing inventory. No one pestered him. And, too, there was always a hundredweight or more of overdue fruits and vegetables among which he was free to choose. He began to consume carrots and broccoli and the like.

He was visited more than once by his mother, who sought to lure him home again. She tried cookies, and then again by bringing along a neighborhood girl with a nice face. They were just shopping, he was told, and the girl had agreed to come along. The boy was friend-ly, offering tea and broccoli to his visitors. He showed them the burns in his desk.

Fourteen

Came the day when he had saved more than a thou-sand dollars, tender bills of green currency that, along with his car, his shoes, and his apartment (room), were bringing him nearer and nearer to something. And then one Tuesday he was called back to the Principal's office, a meeting that took place when the girl (to be described even more fully later on) had just recently begun the violin.

He was a man, the Principal, in early to late middle age with a Kiwanis Club key affixed to his lapel. The boy declined the upholstered chair, preferring to re-main standing when in someone else's domain. He had taken out a cigarette, but had then put it back at the last minute.

"I think I have something," the man said. "And I think it'll make you happy."

The boy put on a naïve expression. "Yes, sir?

"Full scholarship. Our own University of Tennessee. Yes?"

"Good Lord!" the boy emitted. "Whew! Boy howdy. But I planned on paying for it myself."

The man laughed out loud at him. "By collecting tin cans? No, my friend, you have to accept what I've done for you. Or what *we've* done for you, I should have said. And use it where it'll do the most good."

"But . . . but . . ."

"Exactly. Take the money and run."

"But . . ."

"Never mind. She wants to remain anonymous. And she can afford the money, too, believe me."

On his desk, the man had one of those adorable little plastic figurines representing three monkeys sheltering their ears, nose, and lips respectively. He had a globe, a blotter, and for male pupils a wooden paddle about three feet long. By contrast, girls were given reprimands, some of them good enough to summon tears. He had a translucent paperweight holding a frog squatting on a lily pad.

"They'll be pleased, I expect. Your parents?"

"Boy howdy, they will! Was it Mrs. Smitherson?"

"*Smitherton*, she spells it. But she wants to remain anonymous."

He used to cut that woman's lawn. How wonderful she had no notion of what went on inside the boy's darkening head.

Fifteen

In June, he accepted his diploma without demurral

and drove back quickly to his room to pack his things. The weather was good, and his automobile was functioning properly for its age. He threaded his way among a crowd of brand-new alumni wending happily homeward with their diplomas, tassels, and pleased-looking parents who'd all be dead before the century was over. He spotted a girl who seemed appealing to him till he drew nearer. They were so few, the type he hungered for.

In his suitcase he placed two books, a piece of exercise equipment, a flashlight, money, and a wrench and screwdriver. He had a change of clothes, a third book, and enough in his fuel tank, as he believed, to get him to The University of Tennessee.

He did stop at his parents' home and after handing his diploma off to the woman, shared a cup of coffee. Wrong, each had his or her own cup—and a slice of lemon pie. He complimented them on their new sofa and followed his father to the garden where the okra and beans were doing well. (Almost certainly the typical reader doesn't give a squat for these dutiful people without whom he'd be eating uncooked meat and wearing animal skins.)

"Now, son," the man started off, hesitant to offer advice to someone with his own apartment. "Now son, we realize you've done pretty well for yourself so far. *So far.* We do worry about you sometimes, of course. But . . . that's the way it is, I suppose. With parents and so forth."

They shook. The man was less robust than of just a few years earlier, and his hand had brown spots on it. For one brief moment, the brave boy wanted to cry.

The Sun, so steadfast throughout the day, had begun to pale by the time he came into the western suburbs of the university city. So it must have been when Abelard first caught sight of Paris trembling in the distance. Probably it was also like this when Cortés came at last within hailing distance of Tenochtitlan, or when someone first managed to get a truthful view of Mars glimmering in the summer sky. He drove slowly, his hero's eye looking for unfamiliar girls in skirts and shoes. He saw a tall structure with balconies, a department store, dazed-looking people wandering in and out of the many stores that led to the university itself. Slowing, he studied the pedestrians, people with spheres instead of heads, all of them pushed forward, it seemed to him, by a system of pulleys and springs.

He was eighteen years old by this time, an autonomous type who had read perhaps four times the books of his age group. He carried his identification in his wallet along with forty-two dollars in cash, a library card, driver's license, a photo of Gail Russell, and a mnemonic aid for Latin verbs. He still carried the five-inch knife mentioned earlier, also some dozen cigarettes, kitchen matches, and in his back pocket a plastic comb with missing teeth. In the glove compartment he had a bag of fried chicken wings that he had nearly forgotten about. His suit was grey, his belt of leather, and his black shoes had a fair lot of mileage remaining to them still. As to his tie, I have no information as to what he might have been wearing on that day.

He now caught sight of the university itself, an entire city composed of related buildings made from the same limestone. He sought long for a parking space and finally exited the car in front of a massy structure with four regal pennants furling from the architrave. He was received cordially here and asked to complete two forms that disclosed the full amount of his stipend, a more generous sum than he had expected. The registrar, a baldheaded man, somewhat birdlike, clearly had passed a large portion of his time in academic surroundings. The boy was then given over to a blond woman of about thirty-seven who ushered him briskly from the building and pointed him to one of the enormous dormitories that hedged the campus on that side.

"You're going to like it here!" she said cheerfully. "So many things to do!"

Her face was cheerful, too, or even merry, he would have said. Her lipstick was tulip red and her skirt relatively short for her age and weight. He had sometimes seen, if but seldom, women of this kind in his own hometown. For one mad moment, he dreamt of asking her for a date; instead:

"Is there a cafeteria?"

She pointed. "But some of the kids prefer to eat at The Pestle and Whey."

"You married?"

"First of all, you'll want to talk with your hall advisor to get all sorted out. He'll find you a roommate. Of course you can always swap later on. Some of the rooms are for three people."

"Can we have dogs?"

"Oh, I doubt it. But you can always ask!" she answered brightly, closing the door behind him.

The boy went direct to the place, found the elevator, entered, and positioned himself in the forward corner across from a pleased-looking student with an ice cream cone in one hand and a Frisbee in the other. Our hero's assigned room was on the third story, where all sort of postings had been put up along the hall—an offer of football tickets, of transportation to various places, foreign language tutors, and two or three photos of the same girl with her telephone number appended. He approached two students chatting in one of the door-

ways, one of them much heavier than he should have
been.

"Hi!" this one said. "I bet you're K---------."

The boy admitted that he was.

"We're roommates, I guess."

"Good." The boy's suitcase was held together with a
belt, and he had no wish to open it in plain open view.
For though he was increasingly immune to people, he
wasn't yet ready to expose his belongings to the world.

"Hey," his new friend explained, "some of the guys
are going to get some beer a little later on."

His roommate was soft both fore and aft, and though
he might contain more than two hundred fifty pounds,
our hero believed he could have dealt with this person
on the grounds of speed alone. And then, too, the fellow
had already stowed his clothes and typewriter in higgledy-piggledy fashion in the all-too-tiny closet, leaving
little space for K---------'s possessions, which is to say
unless our boy were willing to let his things come into
contact with the other person's.

He dawdled until the students had gone for beer and
then hefted up his tatty luggage and went to the elevator, now occupied by two further individuals who
looked approximately like his roommate.

He drove east and passed through a negro section
possessed of its own special odor. Was he really expected to believe this slovenliness had been inflicted on
them by others? The adjacent neighborhood was mainly
composed of hundred-year-old homes (some with
weather vanes) of the sort he favored. He left the car
(having stopped it first) and ambled off in one direction
(and one direction only) of the complicated city. Suddenly, seeing a policeman, he jumped back out of sight
before recollecting that he had done nothing wrong. He
halted in front of a down-and-out restaurant full of un-

accompanied people sitting quietly in the dark. He
passed an elderly negro with an accordion, and then a
group of three youths with insolent faces. A grocer
dressed in an apron was sweeping the sidewalk in front
of his business. He entered a coffee shop and invested
in a cup of the same. Someone had left a newspaper behind, and it didn't need the boy very long to ferret out a
listing of rooms for rent. Realizing that he would have
to forfeit a good part of his scholarship money for de-
clining the roommate assigned him, he looked for employment opportunities as well. Openings were few. He
did find one position where a person could earn just
under a dollar an hour by setting bowling pins. Or, he
might be hired to care for a woman's cats. Comparative-
ly speaking, he daren't complain about the coffee itself.

He loitered, enjoying the first real autonomy of his
eighteen years. There were some notable faces in that
cafeteria as also among the people trundling past. He
thought that he could see in them some of the personality types described in the novel he was reading. One
man was choleric, another rubicund, and so on.

In the afternoon, he drove back and forth for perhaps
half an hour before finding where a certain room was
said to be available, a place neither too far from campus
nor too near, in an area where the apartment buildings
were tall and narrow and needed each other to keep
from falling over.

He took up his comb, refreshed himself in the rear-
view mirror, and then went and knocked politely at the
paint-flaked door still adorned with last year's Christmas wreath. The woman was also tall and narrow and
had given up on any sort of female appeal. He followed
up the stairs. Her hips were no better than a man's, and
every third or fourth floorboard gave off a painful
sound. Let him have an unsought-for place in which to

live, the lack of sexual distraction, and he planned to be in graduate school in record-breaking time.

The woman proved reasonable and was even willing to consider the boy's proposal that he carry out certain small projects in return for an equally small reduction in the monthly rent. He liked to imagine that a superior person ought be able to live without money altogether, a theory that stayed with him right up until he refueled the car, made a deposit against his first electricity bill, and then sauntered in his arrogant way down to the little family-owned delicatessen situated so conveniently near. It was full of all kinds of things, and he hadn't spent two minutes in that place before he had to reshelve most of the unaffordable items he had added to his cart. In one case, he had actually chosen an imported sausage purely on account of the fog-bound castle shown on the bright green and yellow label. He took out his wallet and looked at its contents. He did have a checking account with his hometown bank, a modest resource once he set off to one side the thousand dollars his father had deposited without the boy's consent. Superior people do not rely on others, and it pleased him to know that most people of his age were willing to do so. Better be dead (he once said to me) than average. Or even just slightly better than average, better to be dead than that.

In the end, he bought a half-gallon of milk, sugar and cereal, mustard, frankfurters, and a few other things, salt and pepper for instance, and enough coffee to last him, as he foolishly believed, for the whole ensuing nine-month period.

Sixteen

He had imagined the university would be housed in one building only. In fact, it often required him several

minutes just to walk from one region of the campus to
another. He did admire the library, a noble structure
that looked to him like something from Augustan
Rome. But more than that, he liked the geology building, a three-story affair constructed out of yard-square
blocks of a cream-colored limestone full of fossils.

He had deemed it proper to start his curriculum with
philosophy, the proper place for beginnings of every
sort. For a teacher, he had expected an elderly sort of
person, a man with a beard, his head of hair turned
white from too much exposure to the shocking truth. In
fact, he found that he had placed his hopes in someone
not greatly older than himself. They looked at each other. He had put himself on the second row, the boy, as if
to say that while he didn't necessarily consider himself
the most gifted person in the class, yet he did view himself positively in that regard.

The room held perhaps twenty students, some of
them, ironically, girls. He showed no reaction when a
brown-headed wench of about five-foot-four came and
sat next to him, and after fuddling about with her
books, bag, pen, and compact, crossed her legs. She was
neatly shod and might be wearing hose. Meanwhile, a
splotch of fluid (sunlight, actually) was edging ever so
slowly across the floor.

He was compassed on all sides by strangers, gregar-
ious types gossiping beneath the general silence.
Framed portraits hung along the wall, Greeks mostly,
together with two Germans the boy identified without
having actually read their work. He had hoped, uselessly, that the professor would *not* waste the first hour de-
scribing what he planned for the course, its purpose,
etiology, and so forth.

Chemistry was better; the place was full of acrid
(even acrimonious) smells that seemed to come from

other worlds. The teacher, too, was a "heavier" type, a grumpy man who hadn't the least wish, judging from him, of ingratiating himself with a congeries of callow students hoping with the least effort to satisfy their science requirement. This one, wasting no time at all, jumped feet-first into the structure of the atom, and before the hour was over, had already begun breaking protons down into still smaller things. The students grew nervous. Many would not be coming back again. Here was a man who wanted to get to the heart of the matter and quickly, too. This man was and is myself.

The boy then strode hurriedly from the east side of campus to west, and after halting long enough for a cigarette, stepped into a classroom packed to the gills with thin boys in thick glasses. Our hero had cajoled the authorities into letting him take a course in astrophysics though he knew almost nothing of mathematics nor of physics itself. (He was to last three days.)

By late afternoon, he had wandered in and out, had scanned multitudes of girls, had bought his books, had visited the library (Tennessee's most excelsior location), and had again reviewed some of the really interesting-looking fossils embedded in the exterior wall of the Geology building.

Came night, his favorite season. Pressing at the window, he could see much, including bits and pieces of his own apartment house reflected in the glass. The window pane was only the thinnest thing but tended to fortify the intellectual membrane that sealed him off from the actual world. And yet, he was in a place where others like himself might be found, ten acres with a million books, a concert hall, scholars full of brains, some of them, and laboratories supplied with instruments as would have entranced the Greeks.

He ran to his coffee and books, turned down the

lamp, arranged himself on his tattered couch—five dollars at the used furniture store—and opened at random to a page on colonial American history in which he could have wandered for years, or until the coffee ran out. He was lucky in other ways as well; the school maintained a radio station that offered good music hour after hour with almost no human interruption. It was here, he said later, here on his little green plastic radio (two dollars) that he first realized there was something in the world even better than literature. Luckier still, they were playing Wagner that night, an instrumental version of *Parsifal* that caused him to look up and blink and then set his book off to one side. Something was happening in that music, a question of forlorn hills, dark clouds, and plangent horns from far away.

He studied, or dallied rather, till past midnight. The assignments seemed to him more apposite to secondary school than to the place to which he had imagined he had come, and he'd finished with them in less than an hour. The music meantime had moved on to Debussy and Ravel, both men quickly claiming permanent lodging in his memory cells.

Grateful too, was he, how history had devised a way for preserving fruits and vegetables in tin cans, a development that let him do without a stove or refrigerator or any other sort of equipment apart from a fork and two spoons. In this fashion he could read with one hand while victualing himself from a can of beans and a wedge of cheese. It left him with a lot of unneeded shelf space that later on he filled with books and papers and chemical reagents of various kinds. One more great good fortune had fallen to him, that the neighborhood pharmacy offered a range of high-purity chemicals needed by him when attempting to replicate certain classic experiments touted in his texts.

Seventeen

Things were better than she knew. Strolling room to room in her new studio, the girl could hum and think thoughts while not colliding with anyone. Any fear that life might not prove to her liking, all such fears now drained away completely. How good the sunlight extruding through lace curtains and how resonant the mauve-colored wallpaper providing scenes of colonial times, a condign apartment for demur people in search of quietness.

Her books were few but made a good appearance when arranged in order of color and size on the window sill. She possessed a five-pound bookend of purple crystal discovered by her on one of her jaunts in the mountains. Her clothes, some thirty outfits of various design, were put away on hangers at equal distance from each other in the closet that also held her cello and music scores. She owned more cosmetics than could be displayed on the bathroom counter space. "They make art out of tin cans," she said. "Me, I make art out of me." She dusted the furniture, finding almost no real dust at all, and then retreated into the next room, where she stripped and threw herself into her exercises, a strenuous regimen requiring never less than an hour and half. She refused to look at herself in the mirror until the routine was finished, and when she did look, she looked with the eye of an art critic. She showered and depilated and then came out into the room and put on a thin layer of a milk-white oil of some nature. It would be another few minutes before her bespoken shampoo took effect, and when it did, her golden hair would seem to have been built from the same materials as the Sun's.

In October, she preferred to practice between the

hours of 5:15 and 7:10, the day waning down at last after a protracted delay. This was the time to take up her
cello, burnish it just a little bit, and then set it up in the
window whence she could acquire, if not an actual
sighting, at least some of the ambiance of the "Smoky
Mountains," so-called, that lay about two hours toward
the east. Next, she took up her wand, and putting herself into an almost sexual position with regard to her
instrument, began with a bit of Bach followed hard upon by one of Haydn's well-known works. The Sun
pounced upon her hair. She was not of this world. Her
future was decided and always had been — to assail the
world with two different forms of beauty, straight out
of a double-barrel shotgun.

Eighteen

On her first day, she came to school in a grey blouse
and rose-madder skirt that was a bit too short. She was
not ashamed of her knees, nor was anyone else, either.
Her shoes were modest enough, the heels elevating her
pelvis by just an inch or so. We know about her face.

She respected the Sun, and when the Professor arrived, he found her stationed on the front row em-
bossed in light. Music isn't everything, and she was required to know about algebra and history as well, not to
mention a *soupçon* of German and/or Italian, according
to her option. The teacher was a presentable sort, and in
view of his evident boredom probably did have the intelligence she expected in instructors of hers. Would he,
or not, pay regard to her two lovely snow-white knees
and equal number of legs that must have taken up a
percent or two of the one-hundred-forty-degree view
available to him? Or was he well-married and immune
to such views?

In the event, they were learning German. It amused

her how in this language all nouns bore uppercase initial letters and how, in accord with her own belief, these people had imputed femininity to the Sun. Attracted, too, the woman was, to the sound of the language, which seemed really to say what it meant to mean. At long last, she was actually learning something. She must return someday and share her knowledge with her people and idiot brother. Not that they would want it, of course. Was she the only student in the class who felt the lesson had come but all too quickly to its end? She was, yes.

She rotated over to the adjoining building at just past ten and sat through a session on music theory, a rather more sophisticated approach than she had ever seen before. She feared that this might give her trouble. She couldn't write fast enough to take down the information. And then, too, she had the impression her fellow students already knew a good deal more than she. Some weren't bothering to take any notes at all. The hour continued for longer than she wanted, and when finally she drifted out into the hall, she was approached by a tall and rather ragged-looking boy, the first male ever to come so near to her in this part of Tennessee.

"Wow!" he said. "This is going to be one tough course!"

The girl looked at him. He was not the one.

"Yes," she said.

"Are you one of the new students?"

"No, I'm eighteen now," she said, turning away. She had to fetch her instrument and then carry it about six hundred yards to her first practice session. The campus wasn't a huge one, not much larger really than her own home town, and yet it awed her that so few acres could hold so many musicians and famous scholars together with so many others who didn't at first strike her as quite so admirable as no doubt they were. Good music was coming from the practice studio, mixed with very bad music coming from passing cars.

Came night, she finished off her grapefruit and got into her jeans and an unclean raincoat that reached to the ground, garments more proper to the farm than to the town. She had a pair of rubber boots with traces of the pigpen on them. Dressed in these, no one could have imagined the woman inside them.

Obliged to attend a welcoming party, she strode in safety to the place and then resorted to the ladies' room, where she could get into her gown and makeup. Two other girls were there already, both of them falling silent the moment she stepped inside. She got into her shoes and gown, a blue affair the color of the sky. It wasn't till she came to her eyeliner, her mascara, and eye shadow that her real artistry came into effect. Her lashes were naturally thick, and she needed only the least bit of lipstick. For ten minutes she went on with it, regarding herself from different angles in the facing mirrors. Other girls were meanwhile coming and going, only one of them daring to interrupt the project.

"Will you be long?"

Sometimes her appearance was simply that of an extraordinary-looking girl of a certain age, height, measurement, serenity, and weight. These things depended upon sunspot activity, one must suppose, relative humidity, atmospheric clarity, or the spiritual condition of the viewer at the time. And sometimes her appearance was better than that.

She moved into the crowd, no one taking notice of her at first. The orchestra was small but good, the singer doing a romantic piece from the 1950s. She must be careful now; a bowl of pink punch was on offer and it might have alcohol in it. Probably she ought never have come in the first place.

It did have alcohol, but not enough to ruin the taste. She saw herself (and her glass-blue gown) reflected in the ice cubes that filled the punchbowl nearly to the rim. She adored all things, provided only they were beautiful enough, her own special morality. There were coils of crepe paper constituting an artificial ceiling of different colors. She must be careful. The dancers and the wine, the music and the people and her certain knowledge of what she must have looked like standing off by herself in the liquid-like darkness of the place. Her nipples were erect.

She came home by taxicab, no doubt a mistake in consideration of the way the driver went on examining her in the rear-view mirror. His glasses were cloudy, and she could see two colloidal views of herself in the lenses. From the compassing hills, signal towers were pulsing with Chinese lanterns, whilst within the passing cars she once or twice caught sight of avid faces sheltering in the dark. Clearly, the ratio here of young people to old entrained dangers all their own.

She stepped hurriedly to her apartment, but then had to return to pay the driver and gather the cello. Within moments she had entered her place, had fed her lizards, and gotten into comfortable shoes. The night was still active, as could be seen between the curtains. What were they doing out there, people who ought to be studying or practicing their instruments? She hadn't come here to fritter away her scholarship money, not with so many generous people invested in her future. Instead, she served herself the little iced cupcake she had filched from the party and prepared a cup of tea.

Left alone, she watered her African violet with an eyedropper and then set out upon Kodály's *Summer Evening*, one of her five or six preferred exercises.

Someday she would play for the Hungarian Emperor. The project took her to just past ten o'clock, at the end of which she arose, exited to the bedroom, and got out of her cerulean gown. Leaving her underwear, she inspected herself in the mirror, a further piece of narcissism and self-criticism habitual with her since the age of twelve.

By seventeen after eleven she had brushed and showered and pared and salved and put herself beneath the sheets. Usually she could defer (if not actually prohibit) the unclean dreams that more and more often sought advantage of her. But not tonight, not after a taste of alcohol, colored lanterns, dancing couples, Kodály, and that encouraging view of herself in her facing mirrors. She really didn't want to do it, but by eleven-forty, still not sleepy, she arranged the pillow on top of herself and wrapped her legs about it as if it were a man.

Nineteen

She was to have four instructors of which only one was demanding enough to do her any good. The students themselves mostly just wanted to feel good about themselves, and to that end went about pretending to be destitute. Others were tormented geniuses with long hair. Twice a week she was made to report to her advisor, a bedraggled man who allowed his dog to attend these sessions. He, too, needed a haircut, and his glasses were held together by the thinnest of little golden wires. He never actually put those glasses to use but allowed them forever to rest midway on his pitted nose. And in short, he was the most admired member of the faculty.

"So you play the harp as well," he testified once the girl had come into his presence. "Is that because they think you'll look real good sitting up there on stage?"

"Probably."

"Ha! You admit it. Well! But can you really cope with that big old instrument?"

The dog, a tiny one, had mounted into the girl's lap and was sniffing at her place.

"Ha. Okay, good, good; now take out your fiddle and let's see what you can do."

Quite well, for an eighteen-year-old in her first semester. The man was pleased. And, too, the Sun that had chosen to follow her about was glinting off the little brass fittings of her buckled shoes. As feared, he fell in love with her all at once.

Twenty

He conducted certain classic experiments (to pick up where I had left off), and by November he had begun to trespass into the more advanced lectures just across the hall where he first saw and was seen by the man who wrote this diary. I let him get away with it (trespassing into my class) until he began to run into trouble with quantum theory. He was unusually well-dressed for what presumably was just another dunderhead youth, and looked as if he had just stepped out of a steam bath after a twenty-mile run. He wore a long-sleeve pale green shirt that bore an insignia on the pocket. He wasn't dangerous-looking, exactly, but at the same time wasn't the type whose mother you'd want carelessly to insult. I called him to the office and sat him down. He had chosen, wisely, the upholstered chair that had served so many of my student interviewees over the years. The other chair was of wood and lacked any sort of cushioning at all. I had used it myself in my own student days and had held on to the thing for sentimental purposes only. The chair actually wobbled on the imperfect floor that had both high places and, con-

sequentially, low ones. As this was *not* the chair he preferred, I've described it in some detail.

"Why are you so impatient at your age to jump into
this quantum business?" I patronizingly inquired.

"How old were you?"

I was nonplussed.

"Right. But you need a bit more mathematics for this
course. What, you don't have enough to do already?
Maybe we aren't asking enough of our students."

"It's enough for most of 'em."

"I ween. And so you wish to become a scientist, is
that how it is?"

"No, sir. I just want to get a head start on it."

"That's nice. But what do you want to do eventually?"

"I'm switching to philosophy next semester."

"So you're abandoning chemistry, then?"

"Yes, sir. I figure I've already learned the main
thing."

"And what is that? I'll need to know."

"That life is just a molecular accident. But I think life
is better than that."

"Alright. But you'd have a better chance for a good
job with chemistry, however."

"I got a job now."

"Washing dishes?"

"No, sir. Landscaping."

"Ah! Now I see why you need philosophy. By the
way, I've noticed how you always sit way in the back of
the room when I'm talking. Why is that?"

"I don't know enough algebra for the front row."

That was it, the moment I chose to give up my con-
descending ways with this boy.

"And so where are you from, actually? If I may ask."

He listed the town, a godforsaken soybean community in the central-east section in what otherwise was a pretty good state. But must I *forever* go on with these sarcasms of mine?

"Can I offer you a cup of coffee, then?" I mooted, nodding toward the well-sooted and highly experienced coffee maker on the hotplate, an article that reminded me of my fourteen months under house arrest. "I'll have to make it from scratch."

"I guess not."

He sat without moving, his two eyes converging on just one of mine. The right one to be precise. Made me nervous, I admit.

"You'll have to forget about everything that's rational or even just commonsensical if you really want to get into quantum stuff."

"That's okay, I don't care about rational chemistry, anyway. Matter of fact, I spit on it."

I moved my papers out of range. "So you plan to be a philosopher who's irrational?"

"Best place for it."

Nonplussed again. A witty quantity. More and more these days, we docents are astounded by the quality of our students, the two or three with promise on the one hand and all the others on the other hands. He continued staring at me, which is to say until his glance diverged off to the side to pick up my oil portrait of Humboldt half visible behind an untidy stack of journals and student papers. I owned, still do, a scale model spectrometer made of gold (brass, actually) which the imbecile thought was real.

"Do you have a girlfriend?" I asked suddenly, without good reason. (He seemed to have everything else.)

"Not yet."

"A quantum girlfriend I think you need, and irrational as well. But I still don't know why you wanted to see me."

"I just wanted to ask. Since everything, no matter how big it is, can always get bigger, can small things always get smaller, no matter how small it is?"

"Well! It stands to reason . . ."

"There's a fellow up in Connecticut has figured out how to break quarks down into some *really* small stuff."

"Interesting." (Nonplussed again.) "But just now I have to get ready for my next class and . . ." I stood at that moment and asked the varlet to come visit me again someday.

Twenty-one

Two hundred miles southeast of here, the girl was slicing open her morning grapefruit, and after covering it in sunflower seeds was gustatorially—she wouldn't want to be seen doing this—was gustatorially devouring her morning calories, some one hundred fifteen of them. She had gained better than two ounces over the last days and had fallen into something closely related to mental depression. And yet, an hour or two on the cello and she had reason to hope those ounces and maybe more might leave her and not come back again. The possibility that somewhere someone was more beautiful than she . . . That hurt. She weighed one hundred twenty-one now, but the perimeter of her bust *still* wasn't twice her waist's.

We were speaking of the boy, six feet two inches tall, somewhat introverted, possessed of superior speed and a good left jab that could have done real damage to any of the local negroes who might be tempted to jump on him in any of the dark alleys that led to school. No one bothered him, however, and after six weeks (at $1.75 per hour) of planting longleaf pines in soil that probably wouldn't sustain them (the University was vain about its grounds) he left science and switched over to philosophy with an emphasis on history. He had read Toynbee (the abridged version, anyway) and had been introduced to Spengler, Evola, and the others. His interest in chemistry wasn't hindered by that, however, and he continued to visit me when he found himself in the vicinity. (Drawn, I believe, as much by the laboratory's peculiar odors as by my perpetual presence in the place.) I had learned to keep a fresh pot of coffee over the Bunsen burner.

"So you've opted out of science, then."

He blushed.

"No, sir. But . . ."

"Yes?"

"Science is about matter and space and so on. *Unconscious* things."

"Unconscious things. Things without spiritual content — is that you mean to say?"

He nodded slowly, his eye at all times on Herr Humboldt.

"Some would say that everything is conscious. Or is the expression of consciousness. You're a philosopher, no?"

"Emerson, you mean?"

"No science without consciousness. Science is merely what goes on in someone's brain, yes?"

"Yes, sir, I know about that. The world is just a mind and the dreams it dreams."

"Makes a person dizzy, no? Thoughts like that?"

"It did at first. But maybe it doesn't matter, if the dreams are good enough."

"And so a fine reproduction is just as good as the real thing?"

"Cheaper, too."

I laughed out loud at the boy. His face was glum — it

always was—and in his right hand he carried three heavy books, not to mention the first-year chemistry text authored by myself.

In December he bought himself a car, an experienced appliance with lots of problems. Having brought it home, he washed and polished it, changed the oil, and carried out other procedures recommended by the blackguard who had sold it to him. The boy had known in advance that he'd be cheated, of course, but had refused to waste time learning how not to be so cheated.

He would drive out into the country, finding it impossible to do any serious thinking anent so much autumnal beauty. Each colored leaf, like every drop of water, contained at least some little trace of everything in the periodic table on his apartment wall. And the hills of Tennessee, representations of aspiration, seemed to offer jumping-off places to better universes. Mahler's music came to mind. He liked to imagine the nature of things in the most ancient times of all, unpredictable fruits and vegetables and a green plashing sea breaking like glass on Cenozoic shores. Time was old.

He drove back slowly to inhabited regions, a discouraging project always. He passed a spate of girls, a smiling race as insubstantial as a specimen of air trapped between one's finger and thumb. They strolled like men, most of them, whereas he had no respect for girls who hadn't learned to move in at least three directions at once.

Eleven weeks into English Literature, he accepted a failing grade in order to get out of it. Truth was, they were indifferent to literature, those people, and were much more dedicated to social rearrangement. Some people were richer than others, some better-looking, some more intelligent—they hated it. So he transferred to Archeology, hoping to share in the excavations then taking place in and around Mycenaean Gla.

He learned to do without sleep, making up for it on weekends. Between days and nights, he preferred the latter. He had a kerosene lamp and a hundred books (one hundred four, actually) on loan from the library. He had a hundred-year-old Cambridge atlas, a copy of Cockayne's *Leechdoms, Wortcunning and Starcraft*, a magnifying glass, a mousetrap, a typewriter, and a slide rule. He had sought a doctor's prescription to keep him awake and another to belay his libido. His room was uncanny, much longer and narrower than need be. He had six suits together with two black shoes that formed a matching pair. Using mirrors, he could trim his own hair. His part-time salary was small, and yet he was able to put a percent of it into an account paying 3.2 percent. But mostly it was the stock market that entranced him, an impossibly ingenious way for feeding off the accomplishments of others.

I never said he didn't have vices, many in fact, as judged by standard values. His arrogance was obscene, and after twenty years of error he had freed himself of compassion on behalf of weak people. And in short, he desired a Spartan world in which power, genius, beauty, and assertion held sway.

He was cold and getting colder, precocious to an unhealthy degree, and immune equally to hostility and friendship alike. No one bothered him, not until the day a pretty girl bumped up against him in the chemistry lab and began apologizing at needless length.

"Oh!" said she. "I'm so sorry!"

"No harm. But I don't plan on getting married."

She left, giving the boy a rueful view of her pretty ass.

But mostly he was absorbed in the uncanny vapor swirling about the chemistry lab. He passed through a green cloud wafting down the hall, a highly vaporous product as bilious and as thin as an equal volume of ordinary atmosphere. He stood at attention as the ten billion little molecules (not the exact number) ran away from each other to the corners of the world.

Twenty-two

He worked his way through a day and a half of mid-level mental depression, and then on Thursday jumped up and reported to class. There were more girls here than other people, all of them "in season," judging by their makeup and kit. There was no question but that ladies' skirts were at least three inches shorter here than in the non-academic world. His eye was keen, and in one case he saw where someone's garter's belt was affixed to the top of someone's hose. This sight, in combination with the girl's serious and rather naïve face, was like a preview of paradise, wounding him to the soul. But he needed to give attention to the lecture, and after a few minutes proved able to do so.

Came noon, he resorted to the cafeteria, a capacious arena full of yet other girls and hoses, lips, and legs and smiles aplenty, and laughter. The food was superb, at least by comparison with his usual groceries. He invested in a piece of meat and, consumed with guilt, consumed it. A man of his type ought never take advantage of people paid to cook, not unless he liked the person and was willing to sit at the same table with her.

It came the hour for him to earn his own salary, a not-unpleasant sort of work that had him planting tulip bulbs in a decorative area that bordered the entryway to campus. He tried to estimate the colors those bulbs would produce and proceeded to organize the planting to replicate the Confederate Flag. He came across tiny animals in the soil who desired to go on living. The Sun was in a granular phase, but he daren't stare at it for long. An hour of it, thoroughly exhausted from his all-too-many activities, he crawled into a shaded area, finished off his soft drink, and lay him down to sleep.

He dozed till almost three o'clock and then ambled over to the concrete-block warehouse where the school's tractors and other equipment were kept. He had some respect for the maintenance workers, a burly people with large hands and unclean fingernails. He had seen one of them lift up a rattlesnake and decollate the thing by using it like a whip. He had respect, too, for the supervisor, though his hands had become soft and pudgy after his years behind the desk. Passing over his timecard, the boy waited to be paid.

"I seen you," the man said. "I shouldn't never ought to have hired you in the first place."

"How come?"

"Sleeping on the job. I don't cotton to that kind of thing."

"Yeah, but I got as much done as anybody else!"

"That right? Then think how much you could do if you didn't work at all."

"Okay, that's what I'll do, then. Will you give me a raise?"

He almost laughed, but chose instead to toss a glance to the atrabilious-looking man dithering with something or another, a broken water pump belike, over at stage right.

"Says he wants a raise. Tell you what, I don't even want to see you over here anymore. Hell, I don't even want to see you anywhere else, either. Not over there and not over here, not in the cafeteria, and not downtown, either. You get my drift? I figured you would."

The boy took his wages and counted it. He could have made better money begging for dimes or polishing the hundred-dollar shoes belonging to fraternity boys.

He returned late to his room and, after listening at the door, leapt inside. No one could see his face or try to speak to him in this holy place. He might be smirched in the filth of higher education, but in his pocket he possessed some forty-one dollars more than the same time last week. A letter was awaiting him, no doubt another naïve missive from his people who *still* imagined they knew what was best for him. He couldn't count the times he had offered them his own advice, which they had always deflected.

He showered and undressed and hung his clothes up to dry. He had intended to jump into Chapter Nine of his chemistry text, and did. Those compounds and elements, they had their quiddities certainly. But was it owing to *will*? No. In all this world (he had decided) it was only what transpired within a choice area of cerebral matter that really mattered. Was there even a hundredweight of such stuff in the entire universe? He returned to his periodic table, a work of genius, his rain-damaged copy gotten for seventy-five cents.

It was raining now. He did so love it, to turn his cherished green leather couch to the window and read and smoke and think in company with a dense grey downpour that promised to obliterate the quotidian world. He had been learning about the extraordinarily complicated events "bookended," he said, by the twentieth-century's two big wars. Fields of dead people, loving couples losing touch with each other, the last surviving copies of so many luscious volumes lying at hazard in the bombed-out streets. He was just twenty years old, but already he ranked "beauty," or "truth," or "the singularity" (some called it), or "god," or the "ineffable," or that undeclared "monster" (others sometimes called it) always lurking just on the other side of the hill; already he ranked these much higher than two-footed things carrying umbrellas in the rain.

"What *is* it with you after all? And why are you so anxious to be the most unhappy man on Earth?"

(He was consulting with his nervous counselor. Me again.)

"I got the best score in class," he said. "So why did you give Duane a higher grade!"

"Why? Because he tried harder."

"And so I get punished for being smart?"

"Get used to it. I had to."

He stood, walked two paces, and then came back. Three books lay in his lap, though I could see the title only of the topmost one.

"Strange taste," I said. (Against my advice, the rectum had been dipping into works on theoretical and practical magic.)

"I like this book!"

"Why is that?"

"Well! He talks about history without putting it through a humanitarian filter."

"How do you mean?"

"Well! He doesn't worry too much if a lot of mediocre people get killed in wars and such."

Oh, boy. Evil by nature, he was appareled that day in a suit of some kind, a poorly-fitting affair that was no worse, however, than what the more advanced members of the faculty affected. His tie was long and ran down into his pants. From the time on his watch, it seemed not to be functioning at all.

His hair was short, shorn with a lawnmower. A slide rule was affixed to his belt while a rosy red kerchief spilled from his vest. His attire was conservative and hilarious both, if not in that order exactly.

"The girls like you?" I asked.

"Naw! One of them maybe."

"Oh?"

"She's an idiot."

"Sorry to hear it. Some of our chemistry and physics girls are pretty smart."

"I've seen 'em."

"I could introduce you."

"I guess not. I just don't have the time. I'm taking seven classes now, as you probably know."

"They don't allow that much."

"Which is not even to mention Chinese."

"Chinese?"

"Yeah, and it's not free, either. Charges ten dollars an hour."

"Who does?"

"That lady. Works at the cafeteria."

"Good Lord. You're getting credit for this, I hope."

"No, sir. I'm not even supposed to be doing it."

"And you're taking boxing lessons on top of everything else?"

"No, sir; I got a gun now."

"And a car I believe?"

"Yes, sir. It's a real old one, though."

"Old as me?"

"No, sir." Suddenly he jumped up, went to the cabinet, and began fuddling with my books. The ash on his cigarette was unduly long by now and was threatening to topple onto a certain eighteenth-century engraving that had cost me dear.

Twenty-three

Slowly, slowly, slowly, our two people were closing in on each other. The times were bad for cattlemen, however, and although the old man had done passably well, the future boded all sorts of bad for people of his kind. Five months earlier, he might have sold his animals on the futures market and now regretted that he hadn't.

This bad news arrived just as the semester was ending. Her parents, always willing to transfer their problems to their first-born, awaited her with increasing cheer as she drew nearer. She did have some money, almost seven hundred dollars saved out of her scholarship award, another three hundred fifty dollars from modeling hosiery, and finally another two hundred seventy dollars from creating a line of painted ceramic dinnerware on offer at tourist outlets. She did *not* have the one hundred thousand offered by a certain pornographic movie producer from Los Angeles, a thin man with a moustache who had come all that way.

She left campus at 7:18 in the morning and arrived back home before noon. The dogs were lethargic, and a space had opened up in the fence where some of the hens had gone off on unauthorized ventures. By contrast, her mother was in the kitchen. The girl went to her, and after handing off her gift of a serving dish with a painted scene on it, tried to reason with her.

"What on Earth are you frettin' about? You still have the timber, don't you? And those bonds?"

"Oh, you can say what you want to, but your father went and sold 'em all. I don't know, I just don't anymore."

"All of them?"

"Down to the last little bit. He said he would, and he did. I knew he would."

"And the timber?"

"I reckon. But you can't get nothing for 'em, not these days of course."

"What are you saying? Timber prices are good. I checked."

"Oh, I don't know. What, you trying to look like Cleopatra? Better not let your father see you like that."

She passed five days on the farm. They didn't care greatly for the sound of her cello, wherefore she practiced in the barn. On Thursday, and specifically in order to see her, her imbecile brother was released from the institution for an indeterminate time. He would sit in the hay, his face covered in a baffled expression as she worked three hours at a time on Vivaldi, Boccherini, and others of the type. She was getting better, no question about it, but was still far from any major orchestra as yet.

She arranged the sale of twenty acres of long-leaf pine on the land bounded by Peabody River in the west, but required the company to leave the hardwoods alone. She specifically protected the walnuts planted twenty-two years earlier, a resource increasingly in demand by Japanese furniture manufacturers. They would not starve, her people, as long as these remained on site. Having gotten seventeen thousand dollars for the pine, she then organized the sale of sixty acres of their neighbor's loblolly for a seven percent commission. She butchered the bull and got a new one with more vim. Finally, the Saturday following, and with the partial help of her befuddled brother, she hefted up the family's two hundred forty-pound hog by means of block and tackle, opened its throat, and drained it dry. She never claimed to have made the sausages herself, instead calling for the help of a little old lady who owed her a favor. (What favor was that? Just keep reading.)

She had also mastered the Boccherini by this time, having ruined her D string in the effort. She could not replace that sort of equipment in the tiny town nor get the cosmetics she required. Nor dared she even to use cosmetics among her family, an unconscionable restriction founded on moral principle. And while she remained celibate, also was she without pity, and craved to lodge herself forever in the memory of every male unlucky enough to see her. Was she to be responsible for the failed marriages that might result? Meantime she continued to have no friends of course, nor did she want any. She would never allow her love, once it had found its target, to run off in other directions.

Friday, she took the night bus back to her apartment, ardent to revisit her books and art prints, her bright patterned quilt, the painted dinnerware she had fashioned for herself on the school's shared kiln. I mention as well the dozen little half-pint canisters, also painted by herself, holding tiny quantities of raisins, figs, and pistachio nuts organized alphabetically by their spelling. But after a half-mile, her cello began to weigh on her, and she was almost tempted to accept the ride offered her by an ignorant-looking red-headed boy prowling the streets at 5:44 a.m. in a pickup truck of the same color.

Her things were as she had left them, which to say extraordinarily well-organized. Had any thief or red-headed intruder broken into her rooms and dared tamper with her possessions, she would have noticed it immediately. Her chameleons were safe. They cherished the security of their converted aquarium as much as she her apartment, though she had to spend a minute distinguishing them from the wallpaper.

She had a wooden filing cabinet, and on top of that a radio that gave off a sizzling sound.

She must now read and absorb four chapters from her text on music theory, the most demanding part of her curriculum. Next, she gathered up her instrument and played (on a faulty D string) the cello parts from five of the Arensky quartets. Her performance was decent, but with the joy of her homecoming having cooled by now, she fell into a mood. People were interacting all over the world, but she was here. She retrieved her mirror, a three-by-five size article that showed only bits and pieces of her face at any time. It did prove she still existed, however.

Twenty-four

It happened that by the third week of their acquaintance, her counselor gave up trying to seduce her. And then on Friday day, he took up his flute and began to play along with her. He said:

"I might just have a slot for you with the Palestrina Group."

She harkened to him.

"He's retiring, their cellist is. Not that he was so wonderful in the first place."

She harkened still.

"It's not a paying position, of course. *And* you'll have to wear fancy clothes."

"I can do that."

"But it will give you some exposure. *Performance* exposure, I'm talking. Both kinds, actually."

They returned to the duet and began playing again.

In the afternoon, she arrived for history class and filled three pages with the same minuscule script she used for letter writing. Letters? She had writ no letters in months. Her attention was fixed rather on making a good grade in music theory. Just then she felt a sadness taking hold, a climatic change in her perspective on life and things. Perfection was difficult, so very so, while everything else was so much easier than that. She could almost understand why people acted as they did. Just now she was watching a group of students slouching across campus, *louche* people always laughing and smiling and passing comments back and forth. By and large, she preferred old to young. City people she avoided.

She spent an hour and a half at a downtown curiosity shop trying to vend her pottery, succeeding only with a middle-aged red-faced woman who went for a cup and saucer bearing an image of angels on them. Never yet had she sold any of her better stuff, never a single piece showing Héloise or Isolde or the gods of India. She *had*, however, earned enough for a D string.

She visited the downtown music shop, loitering there among the cellos and other fine instruments. The salesman, a lewd person of perhaps forty years, caused her to make her way quickly to the adjoining chamber where an enormous harp was stationed among the other stringed things. She dared not go too near, however, lest she be tempted to test it.

The cellos sat off by themselves, the adults, so to speak, at the dinner table. She visited the one she wanted, knowing she'd never have the funds for it. The wood was mellow, and the thing had been built after the German fashion.

"May I help?" asked the attendant. "You look like you might be a cellist yourself!"

Most people focused on her bust; this individual was fascinated by the rods and cones in her unusual eyes.

"No," she said, "actually I'm looking for something for my husband. He'll be along in a moment."

She acquired two, not just one cello string, and arrived home before dark. No one had entered her dwelling, but if someone had, she would have known it right away. No mail, nor did she especially want any. She prepared a meal fit for a prisoner on bread and water and then turned on the old-fashioned radio left by the former tenant. She dithered with it, picking up voices from Utah and Texas and finally a disturbing sound coming to her, she believed, from somewhere in Mexico.

She understood none of it. Meantime her fingers were busy replacing the D string, whereafter she spent almost two hours on Korngold's much-underrated (in my opinion) cello concerto. She undressed, and after judging herself in the mirror, took up and applied a few ounces of depilatory for the purpose of constricting her maiden hair to a triangle with perfect boundaries. She had seen women who shaved themselves entirely, and wanted nothing to do with such people.

It was now that she began to dread her approaching dreams and what they portended. Love, she knew, could be dreadful. Or mayhap, grant someone her meed of paradise.

Twenty-five

Thursday, she shrouded her cello in a blanket and put it away carefully in the back seat of her mentor's high-cost car. The man was behaving decently, though she was growing weary of his affectations. He wanted to be about twenty years old and was full of the gestures and verbalizations that she found exasperating enough in students who really were that age.

"Hey!" he said, once they were some twenty miles from campus. "Hey, you'll knock 'em dead, right? Like, play that Shosty bit, you think?"

She smiled. Or tried to. The day was ringed with hills, smoke spilling from the summits, not a time to be contaminated with conversation. Her attention was for a stretch of hardwoods in the distance, a regiment of skeletons leaning up against one another for support. She identified all sorts of blackbirds loitering among the branches. Meantime the Sun, her own special star, was shuddering visibly in the cold winter sky.

By noon, they had arrived at a private dwelling in the prosperous district of Catonia. Here the homes were of stone, the way she liked them, and here, too, the dogs were allowed to wander, the way she liked them, too. She stood by as her instructor took the cello and, after giving it a final burnish with his handkerchief, threw the instrument insouciantly over his shoulder. He wanted to appear a reckless person, and his hair was gathered in a pigtail. She knew the type.

They were welcomed into a front parlor decorated with four or five pieces of highly modern art and a medieval hearth stacked with realistic logs. The host was a middle-aged person wearing glasses that made his left eye look implausibly large.

"Wonderful!" he said. "Well! And so here we are. People? This is G——— L………," he said, exposing her actual name to the perhaps two dozen persons.

They gathered around, some smiling and one of the men actually kissing her hand. She was introduced to the retiring cellist, a mischievous-looking quantity, quite elderly, who stepped back, looked her up and down, and testified that she was perfect for the group.

"Brilliant!" he said. "A true virtuoso, and not a minute too soon."

They offered wine and hors d'oeuvres, tasty-looking wafers smeared with pastes and other material. Probably she took too many of the things. Though committed to a (very) strict diet, she couldn't resist them. The host was smiling at her. To be hungry, lovely, and gifted, nothing could be better in upper-class eyes.

She had arrived in a business suit incorporating a skirt an inch too short. As pitiless as ever, she wore eye shadow and a blue beret, which isn't even to mention a cameo brooch and two wee earrings seemingly of emerald that sparkled under the chandelier. She deployed a far-away perfume reminiscent of heather. Her face, of course, was serene, and her nose had that intellectual

look that had come down to her from Europe. Your ordinary male, young or old, wanted to lay his head in
her lap. And if she wasn't nervous, it was because she
didn't know how.

Twenty-six

April that year, I was granted a nine-month stay at
Cracow University to provide a course in advanced
(semi-advanced) thermodynamics. Others might have
done a better job of it, but I was the sole candidate willing to come right away and work alongside a translator
who was to be given part of the money. Truth was, I
was impatient for it. Except for my favorite student, I
was sick to death of "higher education" in America and
sick, too, of a great many other things as well.

It proved a good decision. My new students, most of
them, were a serious lot interested in knowledge, a startling experience for me. The city was old and quaint,
and the coffee was good. I met a woman.

My obligation at an end, we spent two weeks, me
and she, in the Hungarian Carpathians and a further
ten days riding horses and gathering mushrooms in the
outskirts of Pfoidem. I returned (alone) to Knoxville the
summer following, not at all surprised to find that in
my absence my students had grown even more infan-
tilized than when I had left them. In this country, I have
seen full professors wrangling for rock concert tickets.

Another month had to go by before my favorite (↑)
student at last saw fit to make his appearance 'neath the
bust of Pallas above my chamber door. He had been
reading too much, and his face was sicklied over. His
clothes were as decent as always, though his accustomed blue tie appeared to have been entwined twice
too often about his neck. His shoes were bad. He carried
two—no, three—books in his right hand, and in his left

a bouquet of weeds which he lay with care upon my tidy desk. The weeds were flowers.

"Thought I'd stop by," he said.

"Yes."

"I was going in this direction anyway."

"And why not? How have you been keeping?"

"I dropped that English course, but Old Man Jensen let me into his Latin class."

"Jensen? That imbecile? He can't even think at the same time. So how many courses are you actually taking these days?"

"Officially?"

"Certainly."

"Just six. But I get to sit in on some other ones. I get to use the telescope, too, over at ---------- hall."

I wanted to cry. He was earnest and bright, and as out-of-place in modern America as if he had woken into Cambrian times.

"Good," I said. "Real good. But how will that help you with your future career?"

"Career?"

See what I mean?

Twenty-seven

After three semesters, the child had accrued a farraginous mass of disparate credits pointing to nothing in particular. Perhaps he wanted to be an anthropologist, a chemist, a philosopher. Or a slum-dweller living amongst the people he preferred, the thriftiest man in America earning three hundred twenty dollars a month while expending just two hundred three of that sum in each such period. An alliterating womanizer in a world without women worth womanizing, a retired boxer who had learned to trim his own hair, a linguist in possession of about two percent of half a dozen languages.

His room was four feet in width, twenty in length, and while it provided no heating or cooking facilities it did contain a five-gallon jug of fresh water and some two score of tin cans holding pre-cooked eatables of various kind. Life was easy. Everything was easy in a university town with bathroom facilities and no intellectual competition worth mentioning.

He had constructed a desk of two-by-six planks laid across two stacks of library books. He frequented the University gymnasium that offered all the bathing and exercise paraphernalia he required. He boasted to me that he practiced irregular verbs—French and Greek—while swimming underwater in the school's Olympic pool. I do not mention the professors he had estranged, nor all the pretty girls he had at first imagined to be appealing. (Having actually gone out with two, or two and a half of these, he had pretty well given up on the gender, and to allay his appetite and knowing what actually girls are made of, had come to think of them as second-hand Christmas presents full of candy and shit.)

He had even begun to listen to the counsel of one of his fellow union members, a raw-bone, lantern-jawed, rubicund, gimlet-eyed, so on and so forth individual who not only owned a pickup truck but used tobacco products as well. It seemed that my favorite student had developed more respect for this individual than for any of his professors who were not me.

"You need a woman," the fellow attested. "I can tell."

"Maybe."

"You don't get some decent pussy once or twice a week, you'll go out of your fucking head."

"You may be right."

"Damned right I'm right! Want some? Pussy?"

The virgin boy stopped what he was doing and listened.

"My wife—okay, she's my ex-wife now—she'll give you all the pussy you can use for fifty bucks a pop. Hell, she even likes people like you. Want me to take you over there sometime?"

"Fifty?"

"Well, maybe you can jew her down some. That lady will suck the juice out of you before you can get it up."

"Fair enough. But I got to go to a concert tonight."

"Concert?"

"Tchaikovsky."

The man laughed uproariously, a tumultuous noise that caused another lout to come and gather around.

Concert: the program was to have begun at seven o'clock, though it needed some time for the audience to seat itself and grow quiet. He had arrived with sixteen dollars in his wallet together with perhaps a dozen pieces of silver change apportioned among his pockets. He had a watch, the same that had come down to him through his people. He had pilfered a boutonniere from his landlady's garden, the sole single example in over two years of having broken the law in even this tiny respect. He had brought a book for the intermission, but knew he was not likely to use it. There were just too many beautiful women all about in clothes and heels. Just then, when things seemed to be proceeding in a positive direction, the boy set eyes on the woman just in front of him, a thirty- or forty-year-old entity dressed in a gown that perturbed him. He didn't fail to notice how the straps indented the milk-colored flesh among her shoulder and neck. Nor were her earlobes to be sneezed at. Already he had fallen into one of those trances that came over him sometimes when he was assailed by music and beauty coalescing on him all at once. More and more as life went on, it was what he lived for.

For just $2.50, the child had reserved a seat on the

eighth row, as good a place as was. Not only had he brought his best blue suit, he was wearing it. Six days earlier, he had given himself a haircut, and his appearance had more or less normalized by this time. From a distance, he looked like a garden-variety concert-attendee with a gloomy mien. And yet, as he couldn't fail to notice, he was not so awful-looking that the women refused absolutely to look his way. Or not the naïve ones, anyway.

The conductor was serious, portly, and bald, the way he liked them, and from his demeanor he seemed not to expect much from the audience when he turned reluctantly to acknowledge the applause. Owing to what was printed on the program, my student had expected Tchaikovsky's Sixth Symphony to start the evening and wasn't greatly surprised therefore when that particular piece was indeed brought forward before the others. The sound was good, pretty good, though the auditorium hadn't especially been built for music. No, actually it was quite good, as the boy reported later. I wasn't there.

The piece was sad, distant, forlorn, the players sitting motionless with eyes cast down. He saw a Japanese violinist, a minuscule woman showing more emotion than that demographic was wont to expose. People were at their best, he said, when collaborating on beauty, a project that caused *them* to be more beautiful, too.

Twenty-eight

On the twenty-seventh of that month, the boy drove down to the original Confederate Capitol to do a bit of research in the Alabama archives. He could just as well have slept in a hotel by this time — he had the money — but preferred his car. It wasn't as uncomfortable as you might suppose, considering the equipment he brought—a sleeping bag, water, a half-dozen apples, the book he had been reading, lantern, revolver, and a short collection of classical recordings to be described later on.

The archivist himself turned out to be a pale sort of individual, very tall and apparently constipated. He had given his life to this sort of work, but the boy didn't fault him for that. The building was full of documents, old ones, and when he spoke of them, there was tenderness in his voice. He pointed out that these letters and papers were all that remained of some really very interesting human beings, better people by a long shot than the current yield.

"Are you here to do some research?" he asked the boy. "Most of our patrons are older, you understand. Genealogy. Property deeds. And your interest is . . . ?"

"I'm interested in genealogy, too. Or genetics, I mean."

"Genetics."

"Yes, sir."

"I see. And I don't suppose you're here to look at Professor Duncan's stuff?"

"Yes, sir."

"Not that you're the first. Discredited, you realize. Years ago. Lost his job."

The child was conducted into a high-ceilinged room adorned with the plaster busts of famous persons. He was not much past twenty years in age, and here he was, conducting research in a far-away city. His pen was full of ink, and he had brought an extra one with him. Because . . .

. . . an unpopular geneticist had died, and his unpublished papers had found a place here, and here only, where today the boy was waiting in dignity for the stuff to be brought to him. He nodded to the person at

the next table, a middle-aged woman bending studiously over a green cardboard carton full of a toy bear and
other memorabilia of various kinds.

"Sorry," she said. "You can't smoke in here."

He apologized. He had expected to be brought a few
inches of printed material and was nonplussed when
several boxes were set before him containing a mass of
letters (some never opened) and what proved to be a
personal diary in three volumes held together with
rubber bands.

Twenty-nine

It seemed to her on Thursday that she had become
even more beautiful than just two days earlier. Her
weight was what it should be, and she had invested in a
sky-blue skirt that must have been tailored with her in
mind. Posing with crossed legs just in front of her floor-
to-ceiling mirror, she couldn't imagine anyone refusing
to look at her. Supplied with that, her books and music,
her pet chameleons, her nuts and raisins, her cosmetics,
her exercise paraphernalia, she could have lived a full
life without leaving her apartment; instead, on the
Monday following, she hefted up her cello and placed it
atop the little wheeled cart devised for her by a certain
trombone player who had delivered it in person to her
door.

The day was warm, and she had put herself into a
pair of short—too short, really—red shorts. Drawing
the cart behind her, the pedestrians tended to make
way for her. Her hair was pretty much the same as the
Sun's and the color of her lips had been chosen with
care from her own collection. She was full of power
without having had to harm anyone ever, perhaps the
single instance of that in recent history.

She went direct to ---- Hall, took the elevator to the

third floor, chose one of the available practice chambers, and closed the door. She had less than a week to prepare for the April concert and her half-hour sonata that would require the best performance of her career.

Her method was peculiar. After reading the whole score from start to finish, she dawdled for a time, allowing the information to "settle," as it were, and as it were to take up a place in her organized head. Next, she tried to imagine what had happened in the *composer's* head, a divine happenstance that occurs sometimes in the life of certain personalities. And then, too, she enjoyed practicing in tight quarters, compassed by thick walls that held the world at bay.

She practiced most diligently, surprised by how the clock ran forward so quickly when in fact it seemed to her that time had almost stopped. To be alone was for her the opposite of being lonely. Her body and soul had cadences of their own.

At noon, she left the building and went to enjoy a cigarette. She was aware of all the people moving past, and when one of them, a baritone whom she faintly knew, smiled at her, she turned and smiled right back. She was courteous to all people, all of them equally unimportant to her. Surely someone somewhere *was* important, or it were better she had never lived.

Two more hours she rehearsed in her tiny cell and then repaired to the "tea room" that had been set aside for the orchestra people. She was invited to join one of the tables, but managed not to notice it. The tea was thin, the way she liked it. Did it hold as many as fifteen calories? She was aroused by the friction between her stockings each time she (slowly) crossed her legs. And yet her appearance was entirely respectable. No one could know what was going on inside her head. She had two sapphires, tiny and green, fixed to her earlobes.

She smoked, her melancholy expression telling that her knowledge of life and dying was far in advance of her age.

"Ten years," she said, "that's all I want. And then I'll send me back home again."

Thirty

He had saved a not inconsiderable amount of money (one thousand four hundred eighty-four dollars) by this time, enough to support himself for four months if it came to that. A letter arrived on Monday. He disliked these things; particularly he disliked his parents inquiring after his finances. (Why were their checks never cashed, etc.) Disliked most of all his father's threat to come and discover his lodging, his foodstuffs, and the wardrobe acquired second-hand from The Salvation Army and other outlets of that kind. (But might not the original owners also have possessed virtues that he put on with their clothing?) His crude furniture, narrow cot, his .32-caliber revolver, barbells made of cement blocks, old-fashioned quilt, framed portraits of Wagner, his wife, and Codreanu — how would the man respond to that? But mostly he regretted that he had advanced beyond his people's range, and they would hate him. And so to preempt their visit, on Wednesday he occupied his dysfunctional automobile and steamed off toward native grounds, taking with him seventeen wild flowers harvested from the lee of the building. He was not unhappy. The day was sheer and bright with resolute clouds moving in the breeze.

On this day, he brought a first-class recording of *Das Lied von der Erde*, allowing it to repeat three times before switching over to other compositions of the same composer. He was moving swiftly through a tableau representative of a certain moment in history, a sight forever unavailable to the historians of the future. ("Historians of the future?" No, he had meant to say historians *living* in the future.) Just now he was capturing visions that he alone would ever witness — a child standing in his own footprints at a precise distance from an old Ford car of a certain color parked at its own special angle, never to be exactly repeated. As to the circular theory of history, no; life was a *kaleidoscope*, he believed, a hurricane of tiny particles brushing up against each other in higgledy-piggledy fashion. Anything might happen.

Thirty miles from home he pulled over, parked, and strode out into a long, level field that, if only he went far enough, would bring him face-to-face with the Sun. Here it was easy to believe that he might actually be the only person in the world, or if he turned, that he might find that the ocean had advanced so far that he was standing in the stuff. People were foolish to imagine that today had aught to say about tomorrow. Anything could and should take place, and he was impatient that it would. A gull flew over, demolishing his dream that he was alone. These are the sort of thoughts that were always scampering about in this boy's head, a way of thinking for which I accept no personal responsibility. On the other hand, after my years in education, I adore *any* sort of thinking.

He arrived at his parents' home at half past the hour. Which hour was that? He never said. His father had fallen asleep in the armchair with his lap full of cigarette ashes. The radio had drifted slightly and was ricocheting back and forth between two weak stations from far away. His mother was in the kitchen, still and forever meddling with the leftovers, the cups and saucers, and like matters.

"Hi," he iterated.

"Oh! You scared me! Why didn't you tell me? Has

something happened? Something bad?"

(He could feel that he was getting bored already.)

"No, no. I just thought I should bring you some flowers. It's time."

"Well gollee, we have flowers! Lots and lots. Your father planted those gladiolas last year, and we always have that crabapple and so forth. And your sister has that African Violet. You need to talk to her. I just don't know. Gracious, I don't remember that suit. Looks good on you, whew. Have you been eating? Well, we finally broke down and bought that new washer. Makes my life a lot easier, that's for sure. Where'd you get that car, honey? You could of bought a good one with all the money we've been sending you. What do you do with all that money, that's what we wonder. Anyway, I suppose you're making real good grades up there. You always do. Don't know where that comes from. Me, I couldn't get past algebra. Why do we have to know that kind of stuff?"

Etcetera.

Thirty-one

Three days later he returned to Knoxville. His apartment was worse than he remembered, bleak beyond repair. And yet he had no choice in this matter. The human race by an enormous majority desired more comfort than was needed or good. His arrogance always increasing, he had determined that it were better never to have lived than turn out to have been an average person. Any person who had, he said, "was doomed to repeat himself."

He returned to his work, finding pleasure in research and reading and finding strange things in archival materials as would have dismayed the ordinary run of people alluded to above. Small wonder they kept this stuff under lock and key.

And so by Tuesday, he had already composed seventeen pages of an unassigned essay on the problem of dysgenics and its manifestations in the modern world. Great help had come to him from the (unpublished) papers of that deceased geneticist who had landed in so much trouble for discussing the human races in terms of certain plants. He found these plausible, the boy, and greeted them in the full-hearted way of the young and naïve and very gifted. He used to stroll about campus accumulating evidence in support of his new theories. No one doubted that cattle had been improved by selective breeding.

He worked for seven days on his paper, neglecting the formal course of studies that could have advanced his resume. Seven, too, was the number of copies he made. Of these, two went into the box under his cot while another he passed over to the one single chemistry professor he seemed actually to respect. The remaining copies he offered to the more humdrum professors he admired less and less each passing day.

Pleased with himself, he now resumed his regular course of studies. He moved from place to place, head held high. As an act of extravagance, he had taken his suits, some of them, to a seamstress, ending up with a scavenged wardrobe that distinguished him as a man of great probable wealth. He seemed to be important and wore a forbidding expression. No one spoke, and he was compassed by a general silence that extended for about eighteen inches on all sides.

By the time he was twenty-two, his work had begun to appear in certain small, transgressive journals loaded with good and bad poetry and the like. And then on Wednesday, while sitting three-fourths asleep in his literature class, he was proffered a note on blue paper

inviting him to see the Dean of Arts and Sciences. He
rose at once and went, determined on this one occasion
at least not to reveal the arrogance that he recognized as
his own worst trait. Having put on a mature expression,
he crossed campus, slowly staring straight ahead.
Gloomy was the Dean, a jowly man with wattle and a
head of hair that looked like pins and needles, or sticks
of wire, or larva gasping for air.

"I've seen your disquisition," the man reported,
holding the pages in the air. "Now, exactly how many
copies of this have you spread about, if I may ask?"

"Five. No, four."

"Four."

"Yes, sir."

"And who exactly were the happy recipients, I wonder? If you don't mind me asking?"

He provided the information—three garden-variety
supernumeraries standing among my own name.

"But they probably haven't read it yet."

"Good, good. Good. Now let's continue on with this
a little bit. Is this a project that you were assigned, or
did it just sort of occur to you? Something you wanted
to get off your chest?"

The boy cast down his eyes. He didn't yearn for
compliments. Or rather he yearned not to so yearn.
Even so, he couldn't altogether keep from smiling.

"Proud of yourself?"

"Naw. Just something I wanted to do."

"Wonderful. And so this is why the state is shelling
out six thousand dollars per annum of taxpayer money
so you can produce this kind of stuff? Great God
A'mighty, boy, this is *exactly* the sort of stuff we're trying to get away from! Us in the South. Who authorized
you to do this, that's mainly what I want to know. Was
it Professor . . . ?" (He used my name.)

"No, sir."

The Dean now brought the paper down out of the air, spread it flat on his yellow blotter, and read aloud, "The best society requires the best demographic."

"Right."

"And that's not what we're doing now? You don't consider yourself part of a good demographic?"

"Me? Sure. But I'm talking about . . ." (He pointed to the outside world.)

"Yes, I had a pretty good idea what you're talking about. Now listen to this, buster, we've been willing to go a long way with you people, a *very* long way. But there's a limit. And you've crossed it. There're *lawyers* in this town. And newspapers. We have parents and other groups. There's the *United States government*. No, my friend, you need to collect your things and *go*. Back to your own people. And today!"

The child was baffled. Instead of the trophy he had expected, the silver platter, the gold-encrusted time-piece, it appeared that he was being hied back to whence he had come! So it was that he came to my office for only the third time in our mutual association, sat without being invited to be so, and for the space of about a minute and half, said nothing.

"They kicked me out."

"What?"

"Kicked me out. No question about it."

"Out?"

"Yes, sir."

"Blimey. Things are getting worse. Because of your paper?" (I lifted the paper, brought it down, and recited some stuff from one of the middle pages.) "Steriliza-tion? Gene therapy? You're lucky they didn't stand you up against the wall. Who kicked you out?"

He gave the name.

"Ach! That imbecile? Consider it a compliment. And so now what?"

"Aw, I don't know. I'm thinking of going to Europe."

"You could stay at my place for a couple of days, if you need to."

"Naw, I got a car."

Thirty-two

Back to s*he,* she who had spent five (5) full hours preparing for her concert and then another ninety minutes with her new mentor, an eighty-year-old veteran of the Cleveland group.

"You do have talent," the woman allowed finally. "How old are you?"

"I'll be twenty in five weeks from now."

"No, how old are you *now*? I've never been good at mathematics."

Both girls laughed. To be sure, the woman was a hag, made much haggier by contrast with the surreal item facing her from about five feet away.

"My God, you're a beauty. Wonder what you would look like in an organdy gown. Blue, I think."

"Depends on the shade. And the lighting. I do best in the Sun. Or late afternoon, anyway."

"Sun, yes."

"I need to have some photos at Shelton Beach. At about three o'clock."

"Yes. Along with your instrument?"

"Or maybe on a horse."

Both girls laughed. Suddenly the hag grew serious. "Don't believe I've ever seen anything like you. You're going to have a miserable life, looking like that. What, you think the world will leave you in peace?"

"Not at first. But I'm going to retire the moment I see

it slipping away."

"And when will that be?"

"Not sure. When I'm twenty-six or -seven, I guess."

"I'm over eighty."

"Oh. And did *you* have a miserable life?"

"No, I was always a hag."

Both girls laughed.

She spent more and more time with the hag in the days that followed, right up until the woman brought out a six-foot golden harp that filled the practice chamber. "If you can do *that*, you can do this," she said.

"I think I'll stay with the cello."

"What did you say just now? Don't you realize what you would look like with a harp? Sitting off to one side with the spotlight on you? Hmm?"

"Oh."

"Exactly. White silk gloves up to the elbow. And I know just the hairdresser."

Thereafter they gave almost as much time to this last-named instrument as to the one the girl had been born to. She learned to play in candlelight, an exasperating exercise that required her to develop extraperception as it were, and larger eyes. And then one day in late July: "I'll be glad when I'm thirty years old!"

"Me, too. But that's not likely."

Both laughed.

Thirty-three

I don't know how long he domiciled in that old car. I do know that the next time I drove past his former apartment, it had become a kennel for two large dogs.

He took almost three thousand dollars with him, I later learned, cash money that accompanied him to a standard midlevel southeastern Tennessee town that lay and today still lies in the shade of the Croatoan

mountain range. It was not so small, that town, that it
didn't boast a music academy, a reputable one actually,
and a community college offering hands-on training in
the manual arts.

Are readers still interested in this person? Ineligible
for higher education, he had reset his career, opting
now to develop his capacity for perfect autonomy. Your
autonomous man, and he only, can think his thoughts,
and in the fullness of time turn governments upside-
down. He studied carpentry therefore, plumbing, weld-
ing, and took a course in one of the Japanese self-
defense arts, which one I don't know.

Having perforce to find a new residence, he had bil-
leted himself in the back room of an automobile repair
shop, where he earned a wage of some sort. It was odd
to see his book hoard piled next to cans of motor oil,
auto parts here and there, and the boy not able to read
or think till after closing time. I used to visit him from
time to time when traveling to the cabin that my previ-
ous and current wives and I even to this day still main-
tain on Lake Peluria. We offered to let him use it, of
course; of course, he declined.

I believe it was during this time that his attention
began to shift over from books to music, the only place
where he could come into touch with the *ineffable*, he
admitted. For much too long, history had focused on
what people did with their hands and feet, neither of
those parts granting him what he most needed. I wasn't
surprised therefore when on my next visit I learned that
he had dipped into his small savings for concert tickets.

He insisted that we travel in his motorized car, a
broken-down manufacture that should have been
turned in fifteen years earlier. Holding to her hat and
purse, my wife of those days said nothing. The town,
too, was largely broken down, featuring mostly aban-

doned warehouses, random dogs, an antique shop with a wooden Indian standing out front. We passed through a district of small but decent homes where the usual nighttime people, young men between about sixteen and maybe twenty-four, were loitering on street corners. The school itself, by contrast a prosperous-looking institution, comprised a half-square-mile of mowed lawns and a dozen brick buildings eventuating in an auditorium with a fountain out front. The lobby was well-appointed and had a display of student artwork offered for purchase. We dithered, having not very much to say to each other. She had been cautioned, my wife, about the boy's personality and how to accommodate it.

"So you're a great Dvořák fan, then, are you?" she contributed.

"Yeah. But it's not me that's great, but him. Anyway, I'm not very good at small talk."

The moment came when the moment should, whereon we drifted down to our places, among the best in the house. How much had our prodigy/vagabond paid for these? The audience was a medley of students and adults, a dignified assemblage thumbing through their printed programs. Had only the music begun a few moments later, the boy might have had time to view a photo of the girl on page eleven.

The conductor, a Latinate sort of man, opened with Tchaikovsky's Fifth, Greg Johnson's favorite of all symphonies. We enjoyed it, too, of course, even if the varlet had to mention (twice) that he preferred the Sixth. He was bending forward, his attention half for the music, half for the players, and the rest for the matron two rows down with the comely breasts. And yet he claimed to have lost interest in such matters.

"Whew," he said.

I had assigned my wife to sit next to him.

"Why," she asked, "do you prefer the Sixth so much?"

"Sssh!" he said. "I'm trying to hear."

The piece ended to applause. It was the sort of evening I particularly enjoy, with civilized, or anyway mostly civilized, spectators, music, adults in adult clothing, and next to me a twenty-two-year-old genius developing at hyper-speed. By the end of the first movement, it was likely he'd be able to read Chinese. And then, too, I had indulged in a foot-tall daiquiri while waiting in the lobby. The ice was of daiquiri, too.

The next symphony brought forth that event, that split-second moment readers have expected. In the intermission, a great golden harp, yes, had been brought onstage and positioned just slightly east of the string section. A phenomenal thing, that instrument, though not so phenomenal as the human exemplar waiting to play it. She was not of this world. A gasp went up from the audience, some of it audible. It needed a second or two before the boy caught sight of it, and another two or three before he was fully cognizant of it. He paled.

"Easy," I said. "It's just a girl."

"Maybe to you."

Thirty-four

He began to frequent the music academy, venturing regularly across town to browse the academy library or loiter on the lawn with its fountains and statuary. He did see her once, once only and at a distance of about fifty or sixty yards. But hardly had time to come to his feet before she had entered one of the buildings.

He consoled himself by broaching up to a much lesser sort of girl in process of mounting her bicycle.

"That girl . . ."

"Forget it."

"The one that was just here, she . . ."

"I know who was just here. But we don't give out her name."

He tried a different tact. "What is *your* name, I wonder?"

"Marsha. Marsha Havelina. I'm in the orchestra, too."

"Really! What do you play?"

"Bassoon."

"Are you telling the truth? When will you be performing next?"

"November. But it won't have a harp in it."

He had expected, wrongly, that she might be flattered by his attention. Proceeding on to the cafeteria, he dredged up enough money for coffee and a salad. The sugar was free, and he stored a dozen little packages of it in his pantaloons. Girls were moving back and forth, the beautiful and mediocre interlarded about equally with each other. He should have been reading or earning money; instead he crossed to the women's dormitory.

"No, she doesn't stay here," he was told. "No, no, we can't give out her name, either."

"Do you even know what it is?"

"Certainly!" She grinned.

It needed another stroll across campus and fifteen more minutes to find the roster with her purported name on it. And a good name, too, although he had already construed a better one for her, a nine-letter designation redolent of the names used by Poe for his own women. She had her "own place," he'd been told, but where was it? Placing himself mentally inside that sanctuary, he sorted through her belongings, her toothbrush and comb(s), her pet chameleon, her shoes and hose. Was he going entirely insane?

"So what are you reading these days?" I asked at our next conference.

"She's got an apartment somewhere. Don't know exactly where. "

"But do you know approximately where?"

"Not exactly."

"Perhaps she's married."

He paled. He had gone back to reading the Greeks, the Ionians mostly, a good diversion that he could carry out among his arts and crafts lessons. He was also being trained in draftsmanship. He had a lot of respect for those canted desks with sixteen square feet of surface area, the well-fibered paper, the inks and precision equipment, and he seemed to have a talent for the work. Just as valuable were the lessons in auto mechanics mandated by his employer, a coarse man with, or rather without, two missing fingers. He didn't care for the boy but understood the importance of educating him to the work.

"Well, I guess you'll be going down to -------- this weekend. What, you got something going on down there?"

"Not yet."

"Well, when you do, you're going to want to know about mechanics. Ha, ha, ha! Am I right?"

The genius was getting just three, sometimes four hours' sleep a night, often rising at early hours to blunder through the darkened shop and make his way out of doors. The Moon glinted gorgeously in the little oil patches that stained the concrete floor, and he spent some time trying to replicate them on notepaper with his set of colored pencils. Perhaps he should have been an artist. No. Instead, he strolled about the block, a place of commerce featuring a government office for unemployed people and a former bakery now used for video rentals. Unemployed? He could cite thousands of pieces of work that needed to be done within a hundred yards.

Saturday, he went again to the music school and, without the needed credential, tried to borrow a book.

"No," said the woman. "Anyway, that old book is all worn out! Look at it."

"So give it to me, then, why don't you? I'll fix it." (He was in the midst of a bookbinding tutorial, the best thing to happen to him since forsaking Knoxville.)

The woman smiled patiently. "No, we have a policy."

He shook his fist at her (not really) and then went and loitered in front of the auditorium till the truth forced him to admit that the girl wasn't there. She never went out at night.

Meantime his car was growing older, and he dared not drive for more than thirty or forty consecutive miles before pulling off the highway to let the engine recuperate. He had his music with him, of course, and tonight the sky was full of low-hanging stars. A town pulled into view, a mostly abandoned place dating from the agriculture age. He passed a barn bending slowly to earth, its hay loft providing sanctuary to the bats running in and out. He bethought him of his grandfather's saying that the allocation of living space was God's privilege, not man's.

He continued through the night.

Thirty-five

She learned that someone, and not for the first time, was searching for her, an annoyance that reinforced her rule not to leave her apartment after dark. And yet—she admitted it—she had herself been searching for someone for quite a long while.

The first week in October, she took part in a double performance of the Debussy and Ravel quartets. Hardly ever did more than fifty persons attend these events, though recently the audience seemed to be increasing. Apart from that, she continued to spend most of her life in her apartment. For her, solitary times were better than having to accede to the social tedium that characterized the town. She would speak when she had to, smile when that was needed, and had actually become friends, or semi-friends anyway, with the laundry woman born seventy-eight years ago to a twelve-year-old mother.

She was provided a cello coach who had grown up in Wilhelmine Germany. And finally, she learned that she had a rival on the cello, a post-graduate androgyne paid to give assistance to those who requested it. (The girl had rather die than take help from someone under the age of fifty.) Had ever this person nursed an idiot or gutted a hog? But mostly it was his popularity among the girls that made him repellant to her. She knew the kind of taste most girls have. In any case, he proved so discomfited by her that she felt obliged to start a conversation, a banal one devoid of controversial elements. She actually gave the "boy" a parting wink, she was that evil.

It extended, her cruelty, to using bits of paisley to test her lizard's ability to run through the color spectrum. Normally, the creature had a pale complexion. Other vocations included herbal remedies, lessons on the harp, and caring for the box of purslane on the window sill. But mostly it was her classical recordings, their physical organization, and the delight of hearing them on the superb machine given her by the assistant director.

The middle of October she was asked to play in a

Haydn program at the home of a rich person in Troizen City. The guests were approximately thirty in number, the children seven, and the waiters three. A snooty young man in a moustache and slacks was continually hovering about, until finally she wrinkled her nose at him, sending him away. She could not fathom why the women, not all of them unlovely, had chosen to wear *pants*. As to their intelligence, she had a pretty good idea about that as well.

Came November and the sort of weather for striding off to school in her purple coat. Dark came earlier these days but still left time for walking along the river bank with a pocket full of raisins for the trout. The Sun, her own special star, lit the way. Sometimes she even trespassed into the woods before quickly coming back out again lest it, too, be full of boys. She sought to converse with squirrels who, however, wanted nothing to do with it. And then at 6:45 to scurry back to her apartment and lock the door.

She knew that she was remarkable and knew, too, that it was slipping from her at about five percent a year. She called for bookkeepers (bookkeepers in the sky) to give some heed at least, perhaps even mention her in the archives of perdurable time.

Thirty-six

There's no doubt but that the boy was spending a disproportionate time in one special section of the library. And so one day in December, with the leaves all umber and orange and mellow and yellow, pumpkins rotting in the fields, and crows mustering in the trees, he inveigled the woman into letting him borrow three several books. Pleased that the Dewey Decimal System was still used in this place, he came quickly to the school's copy of Croyden's *Biteroot Exponentials*, an es-

sential work left in tragic condition. He took it, returning it six days later bound in calfskin with an engraving
on the cover.

"Goodness!" the lady said. "Did *you* do this?"

"I had a bit of spare time."

She had a pretty face and wasn't greatly older than
himself. He didn't want her, however.

For weeks, he had attended all the concerts, but never again saw that "Cynosura" in the title, not till Saturday nineteenth when she was assigned to a part in
Schoenberg's *Verklärte Nacht* at the Seventh Street Auditorium. He read the pronouncement (three times), and
in a sudden access of excitement ran to the car and hied
him back home again to finish his work before the performance.

He had duties awaiting him, a four-wheel-drive
transmission, his woodworking tutorial, the eighteen
bee skeps that needed emptying, plus half-a-dozen other self-imposed projects designed to make him a better
and better angel of his own superior nature. His wardrobe was in good state, and in addition to the some
three thousand one hundred twenty-six dollars he had
put away, he had about fifty in cash that he transferred
daily to whichever pair of trousers he was using at the
time. He had seven or eight ties, all blue, an antique
wristwatch measured in Roman numerals, and a pair of
good, black leather shoes. He was still about six feet,
one and his person was distributed equably over his
substrate frame. No one needed to know about the little
.32-caliber revolver he carried always; they never tried
to interfere with him, anyway.

So equipped, he sallied forth that Saturday evening
and drove forward at high speed with Chausson on the
machine. It was a particular instant in the history of
time, and he was highly conscious, as he always was

when on the road, that he was witnessing it at the first and last possible moment. Soon it would be gone. He followed a blue truck under command of an intoxicated person and then a roadside restaurant framed in neon. He was twenty-three years old, by God, and it were as if he had fifteen sensory organs instead of just the ordinary ones. Moon and night, neon, iridescent advertisements, zero obligations, and a working car.

He parked well off-campus and waited for the recording to finish. He had time, time enough for a cigarette and for critiquing the women pacing along the sidewalk. Given salt and ketchup, he could have devoured all of them. Half of them, anyway. Their sweaters were full of breasts, and by some sort of oversight, their winter coats allowed their legs to show, the devils. What did they want really? He knew what men want, but women? Himself, he didn't like to come within light distance of another male.

And yet, the place was full of such people when he arrived at his usual station. He found himself seated next to a student all dressed up to look as if he were poor. My favorite student, poor in fact, was dressed as for the Paris Opera. Excusing himself politely, he moved two rows nearer to stage right, putting himself no more than about twenty-six feet from where his obsession must soon appear. He counted, getting up to seventy-four before the auditorium darkened at last, the curtain fell, and when it lifted again, as soon it did, some of the world's choicest people were preparing to play. His eye ran to the cello section it had never left.

Oh, good Lord. Alert, unmoving, melancholy, her head lifted, she had been put into a light-blue gown that came down to the floor. Her golden hair could alone have illuminated the hall entire. She did not belong in that group, or any group, or Earth itself. The poor boy was assailed by a sudden pain in the back of his skull and a wish to rise and walk back and forth, or go outside and speak out loud and have a few cigarettes. This thing, this artifact purportedly of flesh . . . He whimpered, bringing unwanted attention down upon himself. As for the audience, these people hadn't even the right to look at her.

He could imagine emplacing the tip of the littlest of his two little fingers in the tiny indenture behind her left ear and fooling with the girlish cilia that resides in that place generally. Hell, he would have been satisfied just to remove one of her shoes before then returning it to her winged foot, and, in short, he was going insane.

I, too, have observed this girl, I have even interviewed her on two occasions. Obviously, no one could be as gorgeous as the boy imagined. On the other hand, she was simply out of this world. She could never be mine, of course, but I thought about her all the same. Like music and flowers, things like that aren't generally allowed to go on for very long.

He reported, the boy, that he endured it until intermission, and then betook himself out to the lobby, and after investing in some white wine, spent the next ten minutes comparing and contrasting the female concertgoers with what they should have been, had only the world been what *it* should have been, too. In short, he compared them to the girl. On the lobby wall, he had meanwhile found a bejeweled baton in a display frame, the very same given to Wagner all those years ago by the notorious King of Bavaria, a man as insane as the boy himself.

Taking his wine with him (he hadn't eaten in fifty hours), he endured the rest of the concert in near silence, disturbing neither the cretin to his left nor the one on his right snoring into his jowls. He counted, getting up to over a thousand, he claimed, before losing count and having to begin again. This time they were performing the violin concerto of Sibelius, a favorite of his, which, however, left his milk-colored divinity with not very much to do. Finally, the program at an end, he hurried to the orchestra pit in hopes the players might dally long enough to give him his chance.

He was desperate. Even so, putting on an insouciant face, he screwed up the courage to drift on down to the cellos where he focused upon a fat girl having some trouble with her instrument and herself.

"Very beautiful playing," he said loudly.

She looked up at him in surprise. Himself, he was a decent-looking male in a suit, and well-spoken, too. A fat girl should be flattered, and she was. She blushed.

"Thank you! But it doesn't have much to do with me, I'm afraid."

"Nonsense."

He glanced to his true purpose, already three-fourths ready to abandon the place. He had a good vantage on her profile, silent, noble, sad, aspirational, elevated, introverted, proud, unapproachable. She stood before him as a living person whereon his heart, as Yeats had so well understood, was "driven wild." This was it, not politics nor economy nor even music, *this* was the point and purpose of life itself. He couldn't take his eyes off her. They were alone now, or almost, while he was falling deeper into a trance that to a spectator must have looked like unmixed imbecility. She turned then, lifted her eyes to him, and spoke calmly in that slow, dark, Southern voice:

"I'm aware of the effect I have on you."

(What!!)

"Can't help it," he said.

"I know. But you're wasting your time."

She was departing. He grabbed for her, missing by four or five feet.

"Can I carry your cello for you?" he asked. "Just to where you're going, I mean?"

She laughed, proving once and for all that her mouth and lips, gums and dentition, uvula, and the rest were in the best condition of hers or anyone else's. It hurt him, her breasts and gown, her upper arms with silver bracelets on them; soon he would be bawling out loud.

"You're very flattering," she admitted. "I do like that in a man. Coffee?"

He thought that he would faint.

Thirty-seven

He fought for the cello and managed to take it over into his own possession. His opportunity arrived at the stairs, where he was allowed to take her upper arm, an extraordinarily good one that more than anything else reveals a woman's age, and conduct her and the cello to the outside world. It was dark out there, and for a minute he couldn't discern her figure from the others moving across campus. This thought came to him: okay, here am I, taking her to have a cup of coffee. Hmm. Never thought it could happen so quickly. Or ever!"

"But is it really her?"

The café was full of youths, and he needed another minute to conduct her back across the road and into an old-fashioned restaurant where some dozen adults were sitting quietly at the tables. It seemed at first that the girl might be willing to sit in plain open view, but he managed to guide her to a booth at the further end of the room. She was not mad at him, not yet, and hadn't yet given any sign of the disgust that he continued from minute to minute to expect.

"Well!" he revealed. "Would you like a cup of coffee?"

"Alright."

"And a slice of cherry pie with cheese and cinnamon on top?"

"Is that what you want?"

"If you'll pay for it."

She laughed. He was making progress. Maybe not a lot of progress, but some. The thought came to him that maybe she was wasn't too wild about ordinary conversation. Meantime he sat there, drenched in the aura of her beauty and the sunrays that formed an ambit that almost, but not quite, reached all the way to him. Came then the coffee.

"May I stir it for you?" he asked.

She laughed again, the third time she had done so. (He never told about the second time.) Indeed, she was able to do her own stirring, and having done so, sat looking back at him calmly.

"You're looking into my eyes?"

"I guess I am."

"But the light isn't right. You have to come close and look from a certain angle. You can see little golden flecks in there sometimes. But I can't just make it happen."

"Good Lord."

"I saw a painting one time that had a sky the same color as my eyes."

Her voice was slow, dark and deep, and came perhaps from Alabama. Some girls are beautiful by drawing on Plato's category, but this girl *was* that category that other girls borrow from.

"I'd like to see that painting."

"I can't remember where I saw it."

"Like to see those little golden flakes, too."

"They're hard to see at night. Okay, but I have to tilt my head a little bit."

And did so, a movement that brought out other features as well, namely the faint blue vein in her throat that ran for a short distance before then plunging into the other material that supported her supernal head. Insane.

"Do you come to all our concerts?" she asked suddenly.

"Yes. Certainly."

"And you drive all that way?"

"Walk."

"You must really like music!"

"It's my second-favorite thing."

"I see. Does your mother know what kind of person you are?"

"She taught me to be nice to girls."

"I like that woman. But how nice are you really?"

"I've already bought you a cup of coffee!"

"You're wasting your time. But would you *die* for me? I don't talk to boys who won't."

"I would if you wanted me to. Do you?"

"Not yet."

Thirty-eight

She had been absent for hours, and by the time she got back, her chameleons were hopping mad. She felt just awful about that. To amend, she watered them with an eyedropper and then added four, maybe five, red ants from her terrarium, the only other livestock her landlady allowed.

She had permitted an unprincipled boy to touch her arm. Annoyed, she bathed and showered, buffed her cello, and put it away where burglars were minimally likely to find it. She hoped to have no sexual-type dreams that night, but suspected that she might. Next, she put on a long-playing recording of medieval chants and went through a few routine exercises. Having squandered the evening, she must now spend an hour or more on her assigned readings. Outside, people were moving back and forth, college students, and shouting from their automobiles.

Who did he think he was, that boy? She did fall off to sleep at about eleven and hardly dreamt at all, or not until just after three in the morning, anyway, when she emerged from bed and had some cigarettes.

Thirty-nine

He walked halfway home before turning and coming back for the car. Did he have fuel enough for the almost thirty mile trip in front of him? Yes, but only just.

There was, of course, no chance he'd get any sleep that night. The room was too short, and his heart was making noises. He rose finally, lit the fire, and began rummaging through a price list of almost-unobtainable Kaiser Motor parts offered at exorbitant prices, a pursuit hardly less arduous than understanding Hegel. He didn't ask for college credit. He was also highly engrossed in a half-year course in printing methods. He appeared to have a vocation for such matters, for machinery and blacksmithing, for lathes and drills and decommissioned typewriters and the like. He had wanted to buy an antique typesetter but had no place to put it. And so thus, aged twenty-three, he left his auto repair job and began to seek a place in which to house his tools and books and weapons and his other possessions needed for personal growth. He owned some one hundred seventy-five or one hundred eighty books by now, not to mention another thirty or forty on semi-permanent loan. They formed walls of truth and wisdom that fenced him off from the outside traffic and the quotidian world.

He tried twice to call the girl but lost nerve each time. And then on Thursday, he picked up a (free) newsletter, and after running down the list, visited five foreclosed homes in the five worst locations. He wanted something of brick, a good foundation, a view if possible. A bit of a yard and possibly a few pieces of furniture unimportant enough to have been left behind. A wood-burning stove to fend off the winter weather. A bathtub, a roof without holes, was that too much for a remarkable person who was so good at taking care of himself? No, and he would have wanted, did want, a desk, a bed, and some other things.

The first place was occupied by a middle-age negress going through a divorce.

"Whose fault," he asked, "is the divorce?"

"Hims! I ain't studyin' no 'vorce! He kin stay here, if that be what he wans! It don't make me no never mind!"

"Children?"

"Some."

The second place was on a hillside that was not so steep that the boy's car couldn't reach it. View, too. He sniffed at it skeptically, kicked the walls, and let his face show how dubious he was. He wanted to be shrewd, knowing how necessary it was for a person's future.

"Very well," he said. "I'll buy it."

"Will?"

"How much does it cost?"

He was told the price.

"What! Seems like too much to me."

"Yeah, never thought I'd get it. You can have that old refrigerator, too."

"What's in it?"

"I know what used to be in it. You paying cash, or what?"

"Who's that!"

"Don't worry. She'll leave if you tell her to."

The boy paid, handing over reluctantly the one thousand seven hundred fifty dollars he would have preferred to invest in cultural materials. It wasn't of brick or stone, the dwelling, but did have an earthen cellar for emergencies and food storage.

He had planned to give the afternoon to cleaning the place, but in the event had to give three whole days to it. An entomologist would have delighted in the attic and cellar both. Nor was it absolutely the case that the roof had no holes in it. It was not till he was trying to sort out his own belongings from those of his prior employer that he received a telephone call relayed to him from next door. The voice was dark and slow and much deeper than was typical for an ordinary girl:

"How can I have any respect for a person who won't even call me! You people! Good grief."

He held out his hand to keep from falling.

"Hi."

"We're doing something this Saturday. Of course I have no way of knowing whether you'd be interested in something like that. Kodály, I believe."

(Already he had, by God, scaled her outer wall and was gazing down on the red tile rooftops of medieval Tours, the first person so far to have done so. His hand was shaky, his knee caps trembling. In fact, he was nervous.)

"Yes! I *am* interested, yes. I am."

"Entirely up to you." (That voice!) "I'll be wearing that gown. But I won't have any solos this time."

"I'll write one for you."

She laughed. He could not view her face, of course,

not from thirty miles away. "What are you wearing at just this moment?" he wanted to ask. Instead he actually did ask: "Starts at seven?"

"Yes. Of course I'll need to leave my place a little earlier than that."

"In order to get there?"

"Yes. And the cello. I don't have that little cart anymore."

"Heavy."

"It can be."

"Doesn't seem so heavy to me."

"Well I reckon not! You can't compare things like that, boys and girls."

"No. My mother told me."

She laughed again, a new record. In fact he actually was beginning to see her across the miles. Coming closer, he beheld her nose.

"I could carry the cello."

"Oh! I couldn't ask that. I don't even actually know you very well, not really."

"What are you wearing just now?" (He had again come near to asking this question.) "I could come to your place at, say, about noontime? Give us lots of time."

"Yes, that sounds like you."

"See? You do know a lot about me after all."

"But are there any *good* things about you? Who can I ask?"

"My mother?"

"Good grief, I need to talk to that woman!"

"Yes," he asked himself, "but why are you interested in me in the first place, hmm?" Soon he would be in the arms of the divinest woman on Earth—was that plausible? Her waist had small circumference, and he could just about sniff the smell of her sunset-colored hair when said hair was spread out across his unclothed chest, and so on.

Forty

He had bought his house, had cleansed and fumigated it, and by Tuesday had transferred a certain quantity of his personal things to his new high place that lay just a few rods below the summit of a hill that itself lay over against one of the elements of the lower Blue Ridge mountain range. The more he saw of it and the more he viewed it from various angles inside and out, the more he liked it almost as well as the places he hadn't the money to pay for.

No, it was a good investment for him, and he had plans for it that will be described more fully later on.

To begin, he sought out a retired man who lived nearby and offered him a small wage that, together with his federal benefits, might make his life a bit less unpleasant. A man of almost eighty, he had seen his share of life, and after two years of imprisonment, three wives, three worthless daughters, two worthless sons, and a ninth person, he was glad for a bit of work in the outside world. The boy was good at masonry, but the old man was better at carpentry, and despite his age could drive a ten-penny nail in just four quick blows. He could ingest a fifth of rum without bad results. He had lost a thumb at some date, but otherwise was whole. They liked each other.

"I want to put a fence around the place," the boy said.

"They's some old lumber over to Pinky's place. He don't want it."

They worked from about nine in the morning till evening fell, and by the end of the month had transformed the property—I must admit it—into a cozy estate with flower beds and a built-in floor-to-ceiling bookcase with enough space left over for months of growth. Seeing this, the boy began to perceive a certain hostility from his neighbors, a gratifying development. He wanted to be a living reproach to everyone who knew him. Finally, at the beginning of the following month, he took out his .32 Beretta and conducted a half-hour's worth of noisy target practice in his half-acre yard. He was still enrolled in the state university, his parents believed, and when he wrote them, as sometimes he did, he had to route the letters through me. For the postmarks, don't you see.

The concert was for Saturday, but by Wednesday he was nervous all over once again. Thursday was unbearable. He purchased a professional haircut and invested $2.50 to have his suit cleaned. He had learned that a certain motor oil was the finest shoe polish in the world. He had a nineteenth-century pocket watch bought at a pittance from one of the pawnshops. His purpose was to live the most brainy, spiritual, sexual, aesthetic, etc., etc., life possible without resorting to the employment stratagems endorsed by mediocre people, a project he was to carry out much better than me. Where did this boy come from?

He had learned to work on his roof while simultaneously thinking about the girl. The old man, unable to climb that far, assisted with block and tackle, hoisting up the inch-thick plywood sheets to the homeowner who tacked them into place. He was thinking of her pertinacious nose, her intelligence, her cello, the single sole woman in all the world for him. She carried him back to golden times, the High Middle Ages, Elizabethan London, Héloïse. Everyone perceived her beauty, but he alone knew what it stood for. And what, pray, was that? A visible expression of woman's essence, not to put too fine a point on it. No wonder people stayed away from her. Her beauty had inhuman aspects.

These were his thoughts when of a sudden it occurred to him that he ought to stop what he was doing and try to replicate those turf-roofed peasant cottages seen in old paintings. (He had little interest in projects that were actually feasible.) A roof of grass, thistles, and sunflowers, and the like. He discussed it with the old man, who listened sadly.

"Real heavy, a roof like that. Going to need a lot of four by fours. And seeds. Lots."

"Flowers, too."

"Whew."

They spent a portion of that entire day talking about it, coming up at about 2:15 with a scheme to fabricate some one hundred twenty flower boxes, each of about seven inches in depth. Having covered the roof with tarpaper, or "felt," as it now was called, those boxes, drilled for water drainage, could be fixed side by side on the rooftop and then filled with soil. The things weighed heavily, and the work to lift them to the roof was the opposite of easy.

When after two weeks, with the child almost completely out of funds, the house at last was ready for his books and things. That was eleven days after the following events had already taken place:

Forty-one

He parked a hundred yards short of her apartment and then went and knocked three times at her deceptively ordinary-looking doorway. He didn't really expect her to be at home at 1:35 in the early afternoon, and so, lacking the key, went and took a seat on the floor further down the hallway. He smoked. He had brought no reading material, but with the sort of mind and imagination possessed by him, he was always able to summon up scenes from history and literature and films that he had seen. He never got bored, a rich compensation for the sort of person he was.

"I do believe you could live a full life in solitary confinement," I told him once.

"If she was with me."

Perhaps he slept. In any case, his next vision was of the girl herself moving toward him cautiously, her figure unmistakable even in the dim.

"Good grief!"

"Hi," he said. "I don't have a key."

"Well, I reckon not!"

"Later, maybe?"

"The performance doesn't even start till seven!"

"That's alright, I'll just sit here. Thinking."

He was allowed into her apartment, the girl actually guiding him by that part of the upper arm analogous to where he had once upon a time guided *her*. Refusing to look at her under artificial light, he went direct to the chameleons, who appeared to have had a bad day of it. Scarlet with indignation, they came forward and pressed their noses against the glass.

"They hate me."

"They don't know you. Neither do I."

"Ask me anything; I'll tell you."

"Alright. Why are you so early?"

"Oh! You *know* why."

"To look at me?"

"*Everybody* wants to look at you."

"That doesn't mean they get to come into my room."

"And help you get to the concert."

"Oh, I see. I wouldn't be able to get there without you."

"You wouldn't go at all, if I had my way."

She looked at him, meditated, took a raisin from its tiny container, and said:

"There're lots of boys who would like to say the things you do. But they never do."

He, too, meditated. To die and be dead, or to capture this thing and enslave her to his heart; for him it would have to be one or the other or nothing at all. He drew near, pleased to see at least some little scintilla of fear showing in her eyes. He could strangle her easily, a fear implicit in women from the remotest times. With their noses almost touching, her lofty one and his that was blunt, he spoke slowly, as slowly as she herself was wont to do.

"I'm going to have you. Now or later."

"Oh, really?"

"I promise."

She turned away. Her pets didn't really need feeding at just that time, but she did it anyway.

He was given a cup of strange tea and then left to himself as the girl adjourned to the next room, where he could hear her fuddling about with one thing and another. She had *not* tossed him from her apartment, not yet. She had much to do, and meanwhile the boy had found a trove of magazines not usually seen in the waiting rooms of doctors, lawyers, dentists, and the like.

By five o'clock, he was at the stove working studiously on a kettle of hot, savory spaghetti. If he could break her diet, mayhap he could break her in other ways as well. She marveled at the smell, seated herself, consumed perhaps two ounces of the stuff, and then put it away for future disposal. She smiled, took a taste of wine, and then returned to her dressing room and closed the door.

She appeared to him in a skirt that came down to just above the knee, a taut thing as green as mint. All his life he had respected tight skirts that require women to take short steps. Apparently she had schooled herself in the art of walking, which is to say moving in three directions at once. Her hips, too, were of his favorite size.

"How did you learn to do that?"

"Be quiet. We're going to be late."

Her blouse, of a lighter green, was adorned with a black opal pin. Her shoes were black and glossy and mounted on heels that caused upper body vibrations. Her hair radiated like sunbeams from her oval head.

"Oh, God."

"You're just overwrought, that's all."

They drove toward Pleuron, a walled city half-hidden behind a rising Moon. He had started the evening with a fine recording of Rachmaninoff's *Isle of the Dead*, a piece beloved by both of them. For four hours, he would have the world's most gorgeous being sitting quietly at his side, her supernal profile shadowed alertly against the night blue sky. He might turn to look at her, but feared she might have already returned to that other universe from which she had come.

Neither spoke. The night was thrumming with insects and lightning flashes, and they could see far-away cities going up in flames. The woods were congested with animals monitoring each other noiselessly from the vantage of their multifarious locations. An airplane crossed overhead. Did they not know, the jaded passengers, what awaited at journey's end? The night was perilous, the boy and girl trying to outrun it in an antique car.

They passed through a district with a leaning silo and a farmhouse with two hounds slumbering on the porch. In a place like this, with very little human activity . . . Could anything be more propitious for spiritual development? No, and when he turned to change the music, he saw the girl was watching him closely. He stopped what he was doing and then, fearing that he might run off the road, came to a stop some eighth of a mile further on. She was encompassed in the night, her eyes only sometimes visible among the passing cars. She was beauty, beauty itself. He wanted to cry. The next words came from her and changed his life forever.

"I didn't know it would be you."

"What?"

"You."

He pulled himself together, or tried to, and then forced the car off into the weeds. He could have used a drink; instead, he ignited two cigarettes and gave one over to the girl, a behavior he had seen one time in a certain movie scene.

"Get married?"

She laughed out loud at him, her eyes this time revealing those little "flecks of gold" discussed between them at an earlier date in their acquaintanceship. To see the flecks more closely, he drew near and then kissed her at last on her red, red lips. She did not draw away. On the contrary, she reached around, gathered his hair and then forced their two heads together in a kind of sudden panic that set his soul on fire. An enormous weight of responsibility now fell down on him.

Forty-two

The concert presumably was a good one, but the two people paid scant attention to it. I seem to picture them there, male and female prototypes instead of two actual creatures starving convulsively for each other as they sat a few inches apart in the dark.

They drove away, saying little as they left town and broke into the outlying countryside. It was darker now, the night a more serious matter than of just two hours earlier. The usual people all were sleeping, dreaming dreams of condemnation for those who stayed awake. Everyone should be sleeping all the time, a philosophy the girl rejected, though the boy did not. He had permitted her to select the music, a cello concerto, to no one's surprise.

They passed a series of advertising signs set up at distances along the right-side roadway, sparkling placards ornamenting the way ahead. Very seldom now did any bats or fireflies flit into the headlights, and seldom did they encounter oncoming traffic, not until a moment later when they managed to dodge a monstrous two-story truck spangled with colored lights. They caught sight of the driver, a neurotic man with eyes that looked like eggs, his lids held open with safety pins.

They went on, right up until the boy turned and looked at her, a golden coin against the velvet night.

"Are you sure?" he asked.

"Oh, yes. I didn't know it till I realized just how fanatical you are. It's what I always wanted."

"And no one was more fanatical than me?"

"No one. You said you'd die for me, didn't you?"

"That's the easy part."

"What else would you do, for example?"

He stopped, pulled the car onto the shoulder and looked at her severely.

"Actually, I'd like to eat you. Eat, eat, eat. Starting at your toes."

"Oh, God."

"Eat you up entirely. Your brain. And everything that comes out of you, too."

"Oh my God, I've never heard anything like that."

Her eyes were closed. Drawing her to him, he kissed her, sucked on her lips, and jabbed his tongue into her as far as it would reach. This time he really was going insane. Both were crying. His wish was to kill her, eat her, suck on her, drink her; instead he left the car, went down the road for a distance, and then came back and pulled her out of the car.

The world had disappeared. He couldn't keep his eye off his amazing prize. They were so near, both of them fighting for oxygen.

"Say this," he demanded hoarsely: "I love you."

"I love you."

He dizzied, sank helplessly to his knees, and pulled the woman down with him. In a view from the treetops, they must have seemed like the original two people. And when she looked at him, she saw that he was looking back at *she*. On the boy's part, he could see not merely *into* her eyes but through them, and into the strange secret workings of a mind that had come down from the remotest times.

"I can see what you're thinking."

"No, you cannot! Nobody can."

She closed her eyes and kept them like that. Even so, he could still attest to her breathing, a panicky sort of business that might easily have resulted from a long run through woods and fields.

"And you're breathing real hard, too. Good."

"I know you're just itching to get on top of me."

"Could I?"

"I need to pee first."

He was astounded. Never in their whole connection had it dawned on him that this particularly entity engaged in such behaviors.

"I'm only human!"

"You don't look human."

"That's because of you. I knew I'd have to be at my best to get *your* attention."

"I'd have loved you no matter what."

She laughed. "You wouldn't have looked at me twice."

"I'd have loved you if only for your music."

"No. That might be five percent of it. But that's all."

She unfastened herself from his entangled arms, stood, and ran off suddenly into the trees to carry out her requirement.

He waited, only then coming aware of music continuing from the car. The orchestra had come down to its best part, a few measures composed by a genius able to imagine a woman like this present one without ever having actually possessed one. The music was superb but could have been better with another cellist. That was when he realized that the girl had run away and was hiding somewhere in the trees.

Of course he went after her. At least three potential pathways were visible, one of them made by ancient Indians, one by deer, and one, he supposed, by *she*. Even so, it was difficult to track her in moonlight of the same exact color as her hair.

"It's quite useless, darling," he called (never in his life had he used that word), "useless to try and hide from me. Especially when I can hear you giggling over there."

"Where do you think I am?"

"I can see your left shoe."

She ran for it, moving at good speed in and out of the shadows. She was fast. Pretty fast. Only now did he understand why she had chosen to dress in forest green. He lit a cigarette which, however, gave only the least light and in no real way helped him find the girl. He hastened back to the car, changed the music over to the second cello concerto of Shostakovich, and turned the volume up. It was the girl's favorite piece, and together with his own presence ought to draw the girl out of the forest, he believed. Two minutes went past.

"The *snakes*, sweetheart. Be very, very careful. This area is full of 'em, you realize."

Two minutes more went by. And then in a voice that didn't come from where he expected:

"Do you still have that gun?"

"Certainly."

"Okay, leave it on the ground and go away."

"You don't know how to use it!"

"Teach me."

"Alright, come on over here, and I'll teach you."

(I know this event did actually take place. It was told to me by both of them independently.)

They arrived back at her apartment at a late hour, or early hour if viewed from the perspective of the actual day. He had not yet tried to mount the girl, and when they reached her door, he sought to shock her by not asking to come inside.

"Well. Goodnight."

(He had a view of her tidy parlor, but couldn't really see into the room with the bed and two colored quilts.)

"Goodnight," she said. "And thank you for taking me."

"No, no, that was my idea."

"My idea, too."

"No, no, just mine."

"I was the one who suggested it."

"Suggest? There's a good deal of difference between suggesting something and actually doing it!"

"You're right, of course. I have to get used to that. It's so late you probably don't even want to come inside."

"I always want to come inside! But you probably have a big day in front of you."

"Yes, so much to do. Too much, really. Well, good-night, then."

"Right."

Left alone, she fed her pets and tried without success to restore their color. She had come through the night, still holding on to her integrity for the nonce. She undressed slowly, exercised briefly, showered — it was two o'clock in the morning — and then got into bed and lay on top of the pillow. No longer did she seek to avert those unseemly dreams that rained down on her from the ceiling. But it wasn't just love she mostly wanted but something else, something that held love as a subset. Whatever it was, she wanted it grievously.

It wasn't till almost four in the morning that her dream arrived at last. She was standing out in the midst of a flowering orchard when she espied a man approaching from the distance.

Forty-three

He arrived back in his hometown just as the car began giving off spumes of smoke. He recognized the cause and believed he'd easily be able to make the repair without assistance.

His head was still full of the girl of course, her legs in hose, her sinister eyes offering a conduit to other lands. A person like himself, no longer afraid of insanity, could see all sorts of things in those eyes — children tossed from the broken walls of erstwhile Troy, Mongols broaching on Kiev, the coming of the Business Age.

"You must learn to stand up to it," she had said. "And don't you dare look away from me!"

But it wasn't till past five in the morning that his mind reverted to the girl's lips and the porcelain white thighs of which he'd seen all too little thus far, a mere glimpse indeed.

The following day he worked with the old man on his garden-roof. Even half-drunk, the fellow could carry decent loads up the ladder, which is to say until they had set up a block and tackle for the project. It was the soil that weighed the most, two hundred twenty-pound loads that had then to be decanted into the innumerable boxes that covered the roof. Some days, the temperature reached ninety-seven degrees, and in early July the boy's money ran dry. He had to borrow one thousand five hundred dollars from the man in order to continue paying him his salary.

"This here is a damn fool thing we're doing," he said. "So I reckon pretty soon everybody else is going to be doing it, too."

"No, just me."

But the best came in August, when, with his mind still primarily on the girl, her arms and teeth, the two men invested in seven hundred fifty tulip bulbs which they implanted one by one in the helter-skelter arrangement on the boy's all-too-heavy rooftop area. Within a week, weeds began to sprout, causing even further trouble for the men.

But now, having embarked upon love-at-a-distance, the boy and girl began writing each other. The fact is, I have inspected some of that correspondence myself. Naturally, the boy needed someone to talk to, and as a tolerant sort of person, not to mention experienced and wise, he chose *me* for his confessor. After all, it was only two or three times each year that I passed through that region.

He was perturbed by her buttermilk thighs, but more than that by her Sun-like face that took advantage of cosmetics without having to rely on them. Sometimes he preferred to see her in the face that Heaven had given her, a sort of church-going experience that put him nose-to-nose with freckles and health and man-destroying smiles. Myself, I compare that face to a certain Syracusan coin seen by me many years ago on a visit to the British Museum.

"Hurts, hurts, hurts!" he said. "I want to *eat* her."

"Don't."

"Eat, eat, eat."

"Just lie with her a few hundred times. That'll take care of it."

"No, it won't."

"And so you're going to skip that part?"

"The whole goddamn thing. Toes and guts, all of it!"

(I had never seen a case like this.)

"All things end," said I.

"No, sir. I'm ruined."

"We're all ruined. Me, I wanted to rule the Western World."

"I suppose I could kill myself. But it's like Schopenhauer said; it wouldn't do a bit of good."

"Myself, I had wanted to create a Confederacy of the Northern Hemisphere. Till I got to know people better."

"Had a hysterectomy when she was seventeen."

"Did she indeed!"

"Her parents don't know, of course."

"I like this girl! When may I interview her?"

"I'll ask her to come see you."

"Tuesday?"

The boy agreed, albeit somewhat reluctantly, I thought. I wanted to take another look at that personality and satisfy myself that she was good enough for the best student, certainly, that *I* had ever had.

Forty-four

They worked diligently, the old man and boy, right up until the tulips began to bloom. Oftimes he could be seen, the younger one, bending over his plants, trying to coax the things into coughing up their flowers. The rain, when it came—it seldom did—would overflow the boxes and run down the underlying tin roof to quench the zinnias positioned to receive it. By this time, he owed the old man more than two thousand two hundred dollars, and there were moments he was tempted to use some of the checks his parents had been sending; instead, he burned them.

His books had by this time all been transferred to his new lodgings, giving him time at last to choose and hang the artworks he wanted, a heterogeneous lot including framed prints of medieval book illustrations, *The Three Musicians* of Rufino Tamayo, and the official portrait of Corneliu Codreanu in full uniform. He had already painted the rooms in various shades of scarlet and purple, a vivid layout that appealed to me but not, probably, to any realtor known to me.

Another peculiarity—he had organized his books by color and size as opposed to subject matter. He had made a catalog of his books, a nineteen-page document penned scrupulously in a sort of *Fraktur*. He also maintained a rotating list of titles borrowed from libraries which had constantly to be brought up to date.

He had a chamber pot by the bed, and instead of an ashtray, a fruit jar full of sand. Day and night, he relocated his revolver from car to home and back again. He lived for efficiency or, as his mentor recognized, for love, art, egotism, and perfection.

He did have a wood-burning stove, but for the most part he took his nutrients straight from the can. Nothing was more obnoxious to him than the need to participate in taxpayer-supplied resources, and yet he was weak enough to visit archives and public libraries and draw water from the county well. Having paid in full for his

dwelling, his monthly charges were rarely above ninety-seven dollars, or not until that day in mid-August
when he invested in a six-pack of Puerto Rican rum and
hurried back home to make himself drunk.

To him, the stuff tasted like the worst kind of medicine, nor did he enjoy the effect it had on him. The old
man put him to bed, but by seven he was lying on the
floor again, still listening to the same music for God
knows how many times.

He was sick, sick in body, brain, mind, soul, head,
the package entire. He wanted to multiply the girl ten
thousand times and consume them all at the same time.
He was crying of course, an increasingly commonplace
experience with him. Was not this the perfect time to
die? To die and be dead and remain that way? Possibly,
but what about the tulips? The unreturned library
books? But far more important than any of this was the
thought of those who might someday hold the girl in
their arms rather than in his. And in short, his wish was
to kill every last living one of them while time as yet
allowed.

Salvation came on sweet Thursday when the girl
summoned him urgently to help salvage her family's
farm. There was nothing wrong with that farm, save
that the owners were getting old. For years they had
wished to make certain improvements about the home,
a project that gave the girl all the reasons she needed to
summon the boy.

He drove forward at high speed, arriving at the farm
before the third act of *Götterdämmerung* had finished. It
was a unique vision that greeted him—the Earth's most
ethereal woman (dressed in trousers and muddy boots)
cavorting with the dog in the forty-acre field that provided forage for the half-dozen cows that hadn't as yet
forsaken the place. She was lying on her back when he

saw her, laughing, the dog tugging on the golden sun-rays that composed her hair. Seeing her there, thrashing about, laughing under the Sun, he was assailed by a hunger as cruel and unremitting as gravity.

No remedy for a person like him. And then she was running toward him in her sloppy pants, her divine face a mess of smiles. "Oh, God," she said, colliding into his arms. They kissed in the open field, none to see them but the dog, the everlasting gnats, and a score of sarcastic crows hooting at them from a distance. The Sun, too, should be mentioned, and the girl's mother, two of the cows, and sundry other life forms who had seen this sort of thing before. He put her on the ground, spread her out, and lay on top of her.

"I'm going to eat you all up now."

"Good."

God, what a face. He could barely go on looking at her, scorched as he was by her fulgent eyes. He could not recall anyone in history who had been given such a privilege, namely to lie athwart a goddess and burrow one's snout in her golden neck.

"Oh, God," she said. "Don't ever let anyone else hold me like this. You promise?"

"I'll kill 'em."

It seemed to content her. He said:

"You're breathing real hard again. Are you excited?"

"What do you think?"

"Even down to your fingertips. Imagine what it's like for me. The most beautiful girl in the whole wide world trembling in my arms. You're like a motor, or something."

"I can't *stand* it."

Suddenly she wrapped her legs about him in the way he had seen in certain pornographic movie scenes.

"Oh, God. *Fuck me.*"

"Your mother's coming."

They leapt up, and as she tried to brush the straw out of her lap, he tried to comb his hair, using for that purpose the fingers of his hand, one of them.

"Morning!" the boy said. "Thought I'd come on down and see if I couldn't, you know, help out a little bit."

"She's not but nineteen."

"And your husband, how's he doing?"

She didn't answer. There was a hollow place in the straw where the boy and girl had been lying. They looked at it.

"Anyway, she's going on over there to Germany, don't you see. Play in one of those orchestras they got over there."

"Romania," the girl amended.

He didn't believe it. To get away from that possibility, he said: "Maybe we should start by painting the barn. Needs it."

"House needs it worse."

In the event, the boy and girl scavenged a half-gallon of linseed oil-based white paint and set to work. The barn must have been a hundred years old and had lots of bald places fore and aft. Even so, it seemed likely to outlast its owners.

"This was my room," the girl said, tapping at a window entangled in vines. My student tried to peer into the room, but the glass gave back only a reflection of his own dour face and not much else.

"This is where you used to do your sleeping?"

"Yes."

"God. Dressed in pajamas. Did you always comb your hair before getting into bed?"

"I suppose."

"Do you still have the comb?"

She laughed. "What, you want to 'eat' that, too?"

"And went to sleep around, what, about ten or eleven o'clock?"

"Why don't we just tuck *you* away in that bed? It's still there. And then you could smell the sheets and whatall."

"And those little pajamas. You didn't really need 'em in the summertime, did you?"

She laughed out loud. In her right hand she held a paintbrush drenched to the hilt in glossy paint. Moving slowly, she returned the brush to the bucket and then turned to face him. They were separated but by inches, and her hair was blazing in the afternoon weather. Her face encompassed just a few square inches that, to his fevered mind, was larger than the sky. Sent here from elsewhere on impermanent loan, she was not a normal human being. They both were breathing uncommonly hard.

"You can do anything to me that you want to," she said. "Anyplace, anytime, anywhere. But it still won't solve our problem, I don't think."

"Our problem?"

"It's worse for me. Been waiting since before I was born. I didn't know it would be you, of course." Suddenly she clutched her own abdomen in both hands, the seat, I suppose, of those yearnings inflicted on her when biology began.

"Beat me."

"No."

"Well, gracious, do something at least!"

They kissed and then adjourned to the field where he put her on the ground and settled her on top of himself. Face up beneath the Sun, he listened to her wants and wishes, a shocking list delivered slowly in dark voice in her Deep South accent. Her scope for passion was even larger than he had hoped.

"You really mean that?"

To shut him up, she kissed him twice and then went on with her confessions, moving deeper and deeper into that female territory that mustn't be revealed to standard people.

"Are you trying to kill me?"

"I will you, if you will me."

"Do me first."

"No! I want you wide awake."

"But what if I don't want you to die?"

"That's what makes it so interesting."

"Alright then. How should I do it?"

"I want you . . ." —and here she began to unbutton her blouse—". . .want you to cut me open and take all the evil out."

"Take it out? I depend upon it!"

She laughed. God alone could know whatall that gorgeous head contained. And then, too, he had been tumescent for three hours and was beginning to suffer.

They did their bit of painting, making a poor job of it, and then drove the family truck into the middle of East Field, where some two or three dozen bales of new-cut straw needed to be taken elsewhere. She was strong enough, the girl, to lift the bundles without assistance and shift them into place. She was enjoying this. The Sun had set her hair on fire, and she hadn't neglected to paint her lips a violent red. This was the time, now, this very moment, to make a photograph of her and paste it away forever in Time's album, an indictment of all future girls.

"My God, you're so beautiful," he said. "How does that make you feel?"

"It's what I was born for. It's so good, sometimes it

makes me want to scream. I'd rather have this for ten minutes than . . . More than anything."

"Well, sure. I understand completely. You're one of the lucky ones."

"No, you. You have me."

Somehow she had cut herself at the base of her thumb, a trivial wound that nevertheless had let a few drops of *ichor* run down into her palm. He availed himself of it, coming forward quickly to lap it up with his tongue.

"You really do love me after all."

He squeezed the wound, creating more beverage for himself. "Love? Not really. No, it's much more than that."

She closed her eyes, ecstatic with that sort of language and the Sun.

Forty-five

Having achieved not very much during his interlude on the farm, the boy drove back slowly toward his own hometown. He moved past a run-down gasoline station where three old men sat shoulder to shoulder, appraising the passing traffic. The boy ran past the place, continuing on to where three roads came together, an *endroit* that in his romantic and much-too-literary mind brought up remembrances of where Oedipus had slain his father. And then, too, he had some particularly direful music playing at just that time on his costly machine.

He turned, came back, took a precaution not to tread on the forked tail of a beagle reminiscing in the Sun, and entered the establishment. He had come for fueling, but instead of that, his all-too-historic mind leapt up in joy when he beheld the quality of the place, a museum it almost were, with jars of candy, tobacco products, and odds and ends of automotive parts displayed beneath a glass countertop whereon three blue-green flies were darting back and forth at unexplained intervals. Perhaps they knew something he did not. Perhaps? Equipped with all those eyes, it were a certainty.

He waited for one of the men to leave the bench and attend to him. Not that the boy, regaled as he was by the smell of turpentine and other kindred fragrances that transported his all-too-nostalgic outlook back to times when a man and his wife knew how to stand on their own four feet and whose typical children knew how to . . . He wasn't impatient in the least.

"Need to get some gasoline," the boy said when finally the attendant stood and came toward him. They looked at one another. The older man was smaller than the younger one, resulting in a momentary disconnection of their eyebeams in the problematic dark.

"You come in here. Now just exactly what is it you want?"

"Need about ten gallons of gasoline."

"Do?"

The man was just too insolent. Neither of them wanted to be there.

"How much is it?"

"Ten gallons, I thought you said!"

"I could pump it myself."

"It ain't hard."

Now finally their eyebeams collided, leaping across the barrier of about half a century. He had seen things, the proprietor, yea, and done things, too. The boy coughed politely, making shortly thereafter the following remark:

"Oil, too."

"That don't surprise me. Two quarts and you get a free package of sunflower seed. You can't do better than that. Nobody can."

The boy grinned weakly, paid, put the seeds in the glove compartment, and pumped the gas himself. He even thought about doling out to himself more fuel than he had paid for, but stopped short when he recollected that he never allowed himself to break the law.

It was past dark when he arrived home again. No one had intruded into his home, nor had he expected it. It had become his habit once or twice a month to take his revolver out into the yard and fire off a few shots at random targets.

No one bothered him except for a certain artistic lady—he knew the type—a bohemian woman of perhaps fifty who stopped by on two occasions to signal approval of his roof and exceptional way of living. Her hair was short, very, she wore a medallion about her neck, and her moccasins had beads on them.

"Wonderful!" she said. "We need people who aren't afraid to act up once and again. Otherwise life is so . . ." She indicated around at the working-class homes of the sub-humans amongst whom she lived. No, she dwelled on top the hill in a chalet of some sort with a mansard roof devoid of flowers, the reward, he supposed, of her cultural sophistication. He could have her if he wanted. But he didn't.

It was warm in Tennessee, enough to cause him to postpone his work till late afternoon. Balancing on the gunnels of the boxes, he weeded his strange garden. His neighbors were accustomed to him by now, but still didn't like him nevertheless.

His rooftop garden: like the world in general, it produced more weeds than anything else. Even so, it pleased him that he had successfully reared a number of *passion flowers*, properly so-called, an ornate growth producing dark purple blooms that spilled over into the adjacent boxes. He couldn't have been more pleased. But wasn't he already sufficiently endowed with passion to resist making a salad of that stuff? Apparently not.

Once more he applied for a loan from the old man, and being denied it, packed his bag and went down into the town to scout about for a job. He described to anyone who would listen his knowledge of Hellenistic philosophy, and on the second day was given the job of walking two small dogs on their daily jaunts. The woman who owned them was old and weak, and he could easily have pushed her over and taken her purse. Instead, he followed her inside and vacuumed her floor.

His next position was at a building site where his ability in moving sticks of lumber lifted his wage to the legally-required level. He was, of course, detested by the other workers, who now were expected to work harder than before. Truth is, they just didn't like him very much. He might even have had to take a beating had not his darling little revolver dropped from his apron one day and lain in plain open view for a few seconds on the cold, hard ground.

Where did he sleep and how did he eat, this puritanical boy with his head full of books? He assayed the women strolling past. And then, finally, during his fourth week in town, he had a dream that he hadn't allowed himself before, a dream of his golden girl standing before him without any clothes on.

I never learned where he passed the nights or took his meals, if any, or the books he read during that period.

Forty-six

He came back home with enough money to make a down payment on his loan. Stunned to have the money

returned to him, the old man began to work more diligently, more persistently, and the rest. Together they
had set up a gazebo out back, this time planting pars-
nips on the roof, a winter food that ought be useful to
them in the weeks to come. Even so, it was not a good
time for the boy. His sweetheart was on tour with the
quartet, and then on Monday his parents came looking
for him.

"And so this is where you live, then," his father noted, his eye roving back and forth across the rooftop development. "We assumed you were in college, your
mother and myself. Just an assumption. We haven't
been provided with your address, actually."

"This is it," the boy said, pointing to the address
etched on the mailbox, a crude affair devised out of a
lard can.

"Dean Jonson is of the opinion that you're not going
to school anymore."

"Oh, honey," his mother said. "You could have told
us."

"No, no; it's alright. He already knows everything,
anyway. Knows a lot more than his professors. He's always been real lucky that way."

"Oh, honey."

They were invited into the home itself and allowed
to choose the sitting places they preferred. The woman's eyes were for the curtains, the man's for the music
recordings arranged fastidiously in the floor-to-ceiling
book cabinet that lay over against the sink and toilet.
That was when the boy's helper entered, trailed by his
mastiff dog, a one hundred eighty-pound manifestation
with a bleary expression. No one spoke, not till the animal mounted the sofa with great effort and posited
himself next to the boy's mother. Even then no one
spoke, not till the laborer took out a plug of tobacco and

inserted it longitudinally into a mouth formed to receive it. His teeth had dropped out long ago, leaving
him to masticate with what was left.

"Oh!" the woman said.

They dined slowly, the five entities, then gathered on
the front porch to listen to the crickets. Two doors
down, a married couple was having a spat, while nearer
at hand someone was singing in a parked truck.

"Oh son, how do you stand it?" the woman asked.
"That's what your father and I would like to know."

"And is he going to introduce us to that girl—that's
primarily what *I* want to know. Otherwise, what are his
plans for the future?"

"We're planting roses next spring," the autodidact
replied.

They left next morning, only to be replaced an hour
later by the rich bohemian woman and her gardener.
She was still wearing the same Hindu medallion, but
this time had dispensed with any and all brassieres. In
the event, her breasts were small but heavy, the sort
that he admired least in the whole wide world. Her
nipples were large as cigarette filters, endangering the
integrity of her sweater.

"See what he's done?" said she to the individual
waiting next to her. "He doesn't mind breaking rules!"
"I'd like to do something like that with our guesthouse.
Not exactly like that, of course."

"Well, ask *him* to do it," the gardener said. "Then I
won't have to."

"Maybe he doesn't have time."

"Ask him. He's standing right there in front of you,
for Christ's sakes."

He hadn't time to answer, the boy hadn't, when yet
another visitor stepped forward to submit a complaint.

"Look, I like music as much as anybody, but . . ."

"Too loud?"

"It just goes on and on and on. What *is* that stuff?"

"Mussorgsky." And then, turning to the woman's gardener: "My friend could do your roof."

"Friend? That ole boy over there? He can't even stand up straight!"

"Oh, never mind. We aren't really sure we want to do it, anyway."

"You used to be sure."

"Oh, shut up, Herb."

"Walking around the way she does. You wouldn't know she's fifty-two years old."

"I would."

And so on.

Came night, he turned the music down. It was thundering, and there was lightning and rain outside, producing an enjoyable noise for people of his particular bent. More than that, it shielded him from the neighborhood noises. He now changed over to a more commensurate sort of music, a Wagner composition also full of stormy noises.

Forty-seven

It continued to thunder the entire night, yea, even unto morning and beyond. Remaining all day inside his cozy cabin, he smoked and read and then, toward noon, put on some of his and the world's best music. It was pleasant here on this hillside, whence he could keep watch on the water-logged clouds and jagged lightning sticks targeting the city down below. Going to the window, he observed a wet dog running for cover where no such cover existed. As to the people themselves, he saw just one, a medieval sort of individual drawing behind him a two-wheel cart containing material that shouldn't be touched by rain.

He napped and then, much refreshed, took out the four several photographs he had inveigled from the girl. The first and earliest of these showed her at about the age of three, whereon, as the poet had written, his heart was "driven wild." Shy in those days, she had never wished to be photographed in the first place. Even then her dress was blue, and her adorable little five-pronged feet had both been fitted with blunt little shoes in which she was expected to meet the world. He could see her walking across the field, her cerulean pinafore exposing two soil-stained knees moving in and out of view whilst chasing bumblebees. He was going insane. Not even oxygen was good enough to touch her skin or abide atop her golden head. He broke out crying.

"I *know* you," a friend had said to him. (He had no friends.) "You've hoarded up the love that belongs to life in general, and given all of it to just one person only!"

"Correct," he said. "And as for you, you can rot for what I care."

He wasn't embarrassed by his approach; on the contrary, he was proud. His habit, he told me, was envisioning the two of them huddled in a blanket at the back of a cave. Cold weather in those days, but they were able to wait it out in each others' arms till April and May and the warmer days to come. Or, he conceived them walking across a long and level field detailed with yellow flowers, her excelsior face on fire from starlight.

He couldn't endure it. He moved to prepare a cup of coffee, but turned and came back before he got that far. For some people it is possible to yearn so deeply for something that time becomes an ordeal, an agony in the brain, a snake in the soul, heart's blood white as paper.

That's essentially what we're dealing with here.

Came night again, the second time in a row. Despite his mental condition, he did sleep for about an hour and fifty minutes before coming awake and striding back and forth among the rooms. He visited the kitchen, poured himself a drink, and then went outside to piss. Having finished with that, he continued to stand in place, exposed to the cool night air. That it was growing cooler in Tennessee he could no longer doubt. He had formed so many plans and projects for the summer that now was ending, not to mention the books and flowers and girl leaving footprints in his brain.

His car was fueled and pointing in the right direction; he did not, however, climb inside it, not immediately anyway. It was his long-standing wish that she might come to *him*, arriving like the Sun, heralded by corybantic stars. His mind then reverted to that wee blue vein that sometimes was visible a couple of millimeters beneath the cream-colored skin behind her knee. No one could possibly be as ethereally beautiful as he imagined her to be. And yet . . .

Departing at just past two in the morning, he drove the necessary miles at high speed, smoking six several cigarettes betimes. Almost nothing was to be seen in his rear-view mirror, a blessing that indulged his hope that the world was inhabited solely by the girl and himself, perhaps a smattering of iridescent birds and not much else. How could the world be so unlike what he wanted, especially in view of how much he wanted it? It was his chief complaint.

He parked as close as possible to the girl's bedroom window, and after changing the music over to her favorite piece, turned the volume up. Either it would summon her to him, or sweeten her dreams at least. A light went on in one of the upper apartments. He let another few moments go by, then left the car and came to her window. He almost thought that he could see her lying face-up in bed. Or thought rather that he could almost see her like that. Daring not to wake her, he loitered there for about two hours till the Sun at last began its all-time routine. God loves people who love like that.

Forty-eight

Sweet dreams indeed, she had passed the night in a fever of womanly desire, even at one point actually putting herself astride her pillow and allowing herself to imagine things. She had been a virgin all her life and was growing thoroughly sick of it, too. Mentally, she was somewhat unwell, and at times imagined she could hear herself producing music from far away.

As noted earlier, her urges were somewhat larger than they should have been, the result of living in a land where summer heat was as persistent as it was. A serene sort of person, lofty and sad, a first-class mind with musical talent . . . No one knew what really went on in that head.

In mid-September she was made to go on tour with her quartet, coming back nine days later with an award and two marriage proposals, one of them a plausible offer on behalf of a forty-year-old divorced man who attended all three of the concerts that took place in Micala.

"He was nice," she told the boy. "A gentleman. Tall and brawny, and likes music, too."

"Damn you."

"How does that make you feel?" (She came nearer, her eyes full of filth.)

"I can see what you're going through. Me with someone else. I can see it in your face."

"Trying to drive me insane?"

"Just up to the edge."

"I suppose you think you're safe as long as we're in a crowd?"

"Well, I sure wouldn't talk this way if we were alone. Just think what you might do!"

"I do think about it. All the time."

"Good."

This, I suppose, was the sort of language that brought the boy to visit me at my lake home the first week of everyone's favorite month, October to be more precise. No one adores that season more than those who have only a limited number of them in store. Dogs were calling, the perch were feeding, and the wind was full of uncollected apples decaying on the stem. As to the actual leaves, they were transitioning from gold to lacework, revealing their veins by hundreds of millions. This was the time my special student came riding up in his worthless car. I hadn't seen him in months, the exact same period during which he appeared to have grown a little bit older. His car was older, too. We nodded each to each and then adjourned quickly to the den in order to speak.

"I think he exaggerates," the boy revealed. "Spengler. But he's right about a whole host of things."

"Oh? Which are those?"

He preferred to change the subject.

"We're also getting along a lot better now. That girl I told you about."

"Relieved to hear it."

"Driving me out of my mind! But she doesn't mean it."

"It's a problem. Boys and girls."

"Can't sleep."

"I see. Have you lain with her yet?"

"No, sir."

"Why not?"

"I will, I will. But that's not the problem. She'll still be . . ."

"Yes?"

"She has her own way of looking at things."

"And you don't know what those ways are."

"Right. What is she thinking when she's playing on that harp? She won't tell me.

"She *can't* tell you, for God's sakes! I don't even know what *you're* thinking, and we're both men! Or I am, anyway. What, you expect to break through the girl/boy barrier? You can just forget about that."

"Not fair."

I broke out laughing. Couldn't help it. "So you want to *unite* with her, is that what it is? Like two amoebas coming together to form one business? Forget it. The albumin and yoke of one egg, as Plato said?"

"But . . ."

"Yes, yes, I've seen her."

"And so I'm supposed to go through my whole life . . ."

"Yep, that's right, the whole thing, and without ever being one hundred percent completely happy. That's how things tend to be."

"But . . ."

"Yes, I know. But people don't get what they deserve, especially not when they deserve a lot."

"Yeah, but she deserves it even more than me!"

"Very sad. Sad things have a way of being everything. Marry her, nail her three times daily" — and here I sought to tell him about his first attempt at love-making* — "and then get you back to what you were doing. Metaphysics, is it now? Or die. You can always do that."

---

* Think of it as if you were writing a novel. If the first page be good, the rest follows.

We drank, red wine for the most part. It needed another half-hour before the varlet had calmed enough to proceed to my three-wall bookcase and chase down the five volumes I'd recently added to my slowly cumulating set of Rosenthal's translation of Tabari. Intellect alone (mixed with intransigence) could have saved this child's soul, though I was sure it wouldn't.

"Naw, I don't guess I'm ready to die yet," he said after a time. "I still think I have possibilities."

"Possibilities are without number. It's *probabilities* that tend to be thin. Remember, it's always just the present time that's awful; the rest is fine."

"Yeah, but . . ."

"Women are only women, after all. *Correlative allotropes* we call them, those of us. Individuals of the same nature, but with unlike forms. What, you think a woman's appearance is a fair representation of her character?"

"No! Of course not. It's just a reflection of *my* character, I suppose. Meantime I think I'm going insane."

"Nothing wrong with that."

"Nothing wrong with going insane?"

"Nothing wrong with suspecting it."

Forty-nine

He went back to what he was doing. He will have garnered a lot of attention by now for his peculiar home, enough for his method to have been copied in at least two other places, one on this side of town and one the other.

"You should have applied for a patent!" someone suggested.

Weeds were a problem. German, too, with its endless prefixes running back and forth. He could not fathom the mindset of these people. Busy was he, too, with the girl, who possessed him like a fist tightening around his brain. He cried frequently. He went outside at night and walked about. He had constantly to put on fresh sheets, and to keep himself respectable he had begun using a professional barber. His money running low, he actually bought a real suit, a dark blue affair in compliance with current fashions.

He had a good experience that afternoon while driving about the city. A home had been put up for sale, its contents brought out and made available to bargain-hunters. He went at once for the books, of course, but finding nothing worthy of himself, he gravitated to a good selection of household tools spread out on a table. His eyes hit upon a wrench, a heavy-duty artifact that should have cost more than that. Exalted by this find, he chose a jar of plumbing washers, an eighteen-inch screwdriver, five drill bits (one of them exceedingly tiny), and a dozen sparkplugs in perfect condition. Moving among the wares, he began to hum a segment from Debussy, carrying it off in his incompetent way. No one loved music more than he, and no one had less ability in that special skill. He saw then an outboard motor for sale, an antique Evinrude in salvageable condition. Three horsepower indeed, the thing couldn't have propelled even the smallest skiff beyond five knots an hour.

"I'd like to purchase this outboard motor," he had said.

"I don't know why. Not any good. Never was any good."

"Maybe I can fix it up."

"Don't know why. Hadn't got but three horsepower in it. Probably down to about one horsepower now."

"Perhaps. But I wouldn't underestimate a horse."

They looked at each other. The fellow was large

enough that the boy chose not to underestimate him, either.

"Give you a dollar for it. One horse, one dollar."

"Five dollars."

"What did you say? Nobody's going to pay that!"

"I'd rather throw it away."

"Okay, just tell me where, okay?"

"I'll throw it where you can't find it! I will."

"Here, let me dispose of it for you."

"You come around, saying things about my books. Most of the people around here are real nice people."

"I used to be nice."

"What happened?"

"Prices. Everybody wants too much money for their stuff. Now you take this motor . . ."

"Good God A'mighty. Alright, I tell you what, just take it. Take it right now! I don't want to see it anymore. Don't want to see you, either."

"Fair enough. Help me carry it to the car, okay?"

In the end, he paid two dollars and managed easily enough under his own power to transport it to the car. A million years of evolution and industrial progress had been needed to build this machine, and yet he'd been able to possess himself of it in under three minutes and for what even by his standards was a pittance. He had further pittances in his wallet at that moment wherefore he decided to resume his tour of the town. The afternoon was bright, and October was in season.

He expected to see girls in their autumn dresses; instead, falling under the excellent music that perpetually filled his car, it began to seem to him that the town was empty, no people anywhere. How odd all things were! Perhaps nothing existed. Or perhaps he was alone, and all things else, buildings and people and the rest, were but exudations of his own unhealthy mind. He had always suspected some such thing.

He parked, left the car, and tried to enter an office building that ran up into the sky for a great distance. He was sick, had a headache, and was close to vomiting. Happily, his car was approximately where he had left it, and he was able to pick his way home at half speed. His bed, too, was where it should be, thank goodness.

He slept for possibly five hours, awakening in the dark to the sound of primitive music issuing from a passing car. He had determined that it was time to get into his shoes and was dismayed to learn that he had them on already. He yearned for rain, rain to quell the ambient noises, yea, and thunder, too. What was she doing just now, the girl? Going through her toiletries? Nibbling on cashews and artichoke hearts? And why, when he turned around, was she not lying on the bed with arms outstretched? He was angry about almost everything, and never throughout his whole life had he been able to understand why the world was organized the way it was.

He forced down a pint of potato soup followed by a few other nutrients not worth itemizing. His illness had by no means passed away, and when he returned to bed he had trouble putting himself into position. Came then the rain.

The rain! The rain! They loved it equally, the hollyhocks and he. He dreamt he was captain of an eighteenth-century sailing vessel daunted by waves and high winds, and then next that he was keeping dark vigil from the walls of medieval Pskov. But these were only-too-familiar to him, these old dreams, and he choose to shut them down.

He did not wish to dream about the girl, not at this time. He had been crying and yearning and moaning for the past three days, a time-consuming effort that had left no time for his rooftop garden. Further, he had received a petition, a two-page document asking him to reconsider the project. Worse, he had read almost nothing during this time, and his funds were running low.

"Ah, me," he said, "no one suffers the way I do. The price of integrity, I suppose."

That was when he recognized that someone or something was in bed with him. He screamed.

"Hush!" she said.

Fifty

And when someday the Moon falls into the sea, he will still have had this.

"Hush. I was worried."

"Oh, God."

She was laughing in the dark. He reached for her, horrified to find that she was undressed, or above the waist at any rate.

"Hey! You don't seem to have any clothes on!"

"I got tired of waiting. And besides, I was worried."

"Worried!"

"All this rain. And you never write anymore."

"But ... But ..."

"Harold [trombone player] brought me. He knew I was worried."

"But ..."

"I don't have anything *below* my waist, either."

Her flesh, he later admitted, was as a superfine gold in which the largest unresolved grains were no larger than some of the smallest grains ever known, the interior of a honeydew melon, strangest of all things. He was weeping of course, but this time he had the girl to console him. Anyone seeing this process from afar would have reported the boy insane. With two hands only, he could evaluate *the entire surface* of that entity within just moments.

"Oh, God."

"No, baby; it's going to be alright."

"I can't breathe!"

It was true she had nothing below the waist. This was unfamiliar territory to him, though he had done some reading on the subject.

"I have to go back tomorrow."

"Nude?"

She laughed out loud, laughing in the dark. Her hands also were occupied, causing her on one occasion to emit an expression of real surprise.

"Oh!"

"Well, I guess I'd better get on back," the trombonist said, moving quickly to the door.

It was still raining out there, and would remain dark for hours more.

He came awake before she did. Allied to the Sun, her unnatural hair looked like gamma rays scattered equally across the pillow and himself. He had been an adult since seventeen, and after last night, must henceforward be seen as a fully-fledged grown-up person in the opinion of everyone.

"Oh, baby," he opined.

"Darling."

(Alright, let time come to a stop. History could get no better, and from now on "progress," men call it, would be the worst thing possible.)

"Oh, baby; I want to stay here forever."

"You'd get bored."

"What!"

He lifted a tangle of gamma rays and managed to get about a foot of it into his mouth and throat. A little help and he could have drawn the whole person into his personal self. Better she had never existed than they be hived off from each other by time and space. Or that they might die and their souls never find each other in a universe that wasn't already awful enough but must forever go on getting larger.

"We don't have much time."

"I know. But we have this."

"Yes."

"And no one can take it away from us."

"Yes. It's been *inscribed*."

"We're so lucky. Think of all those people . . ."

"It's not luck! We deserve it."

"You deserve it. Not me."

"Oh, good Lord. Look at you! Routine-type people just don't look like that!"

"It was an accident."

"It was not an accident! It's a . . . *teleology*. A force that started out long, long, long ago."

She came nearer, saying:

"Maybe."

"It happened with Helen and it happened with . . ." (He mentioned another ancient Greek personality unknown to me.) "That was the last time."

"I didn't know it would be you."

"No, I had to force it."

"The more you want me, the more I want you to want me more."

"How much do I have to want you?"

"Till you can't stand it."

"It's already that way!"

"No, you haven't even started. You'll learn, you'll learn."

"Look, I'm the one who started this whole thing in the first place!"

"What if you hadn't?"

"Well! You would have had to settle for one of those people."

"No, no, no, just no. I would have gone back home and looked after my brother and cows."

"I don't think so! After thirty or forty of those people had asked you to marry them, you would have."

"That's the most ridiculous thing I ever heard! Anyway, I don't plan on living that long."

"So who will take care of the cows?"

She had to laugh. More beautiful that moment than ever, he photographed her with his mind.

They played for the rest of that morning and then reluctantly rose up out of bed and went to look at the rooftop garden. The Sun, enthralled with the girl, smote her hair, elbows, eyes, and the tip of her perspicacious nose. She spent a long while staring up sadly at the weeds in his garden. A car passed by, the driver hypnotized by the vision of the girl dressed in a blanket, a pair of earrings and high-heel shoes. They returned to the house.

All his life, he had wanted to sit at his desk with regular cups of coffee fetched to him by the world's most beautiful woman; instead, she took his left ear between her thumb and index finger and led him back to bed. Neither of these two people was absolutely normal, especially not her and especially not him. He seemed to have stirred up a hornet's nest inside her.

"It was like sitting in an electric chair!" the boy described it.

"I know, 1 know," she said, soothing him. "But it's even worse for me."

Whether this were lovemaking or a form of jousting or murder by mutual demand, I can't say. Wasn't there.

And yet by two o'clock she was washing dishes,

humming, sweeping the floor, and things of that kind. Dressed as she was in her towel-like robe, she looked more than ever like a figment out of literature, an educated Calypso to enslave certain types of men. And in short, she wasn't entirely human. That was when she stopped to watch him philosophizing pessimistically at his pitted desk. He was aware of a certain stasis in the ambience, and outside, the noiseless Sun dispensing life and motion to those below. He heard a truck laboring up a hill, a barking dog, collisions in the dust, a portentous voice from far away. Time had come to a stop, riveting them to the beginning and endpoint of a glance. How strange. Nothing happened, and yet, looking back upon it from a great distance, the boy (no longer a "boy") was to list this moment the very sweetest of his long and wistful career.

She left that afternoon, traveling by bus in clothes and cosmetics chosen to neutralize her beauty. Her baggage was small, holding not much more than a pound of makeup, book, mirror, and underwear, together with about thirty dollars' worth of cash. She traveled like a Bedouin, a free-range woman with one great destiny. She had no need of abortifacients, of course, owing to her elective surgery of some years earlier.

"I mustn't have children. The only love I want is a love between *equals*," she told me once.

"And where will you find such a thing?" I asked, aroused.

"Well, I did."

"Oh, my gosh, that's just about the nicest thing anyone ever said to me!"

We both broke out laughing. Her eyes gleamed with a glycerin of some kind, and her teeth were white. It hurt me, no lie, each and every time I saw her.

"I tell you the truth, lady, I may be three times your age, but I'd so much like to . . ."

"No, no, no, no. Hush, or I won't be able to come here anymore."

Fifty-one

He needed time to heal. Weakened by the woman's embrace, he drifted both spiritually and physically throughout the house and field. So it must have been with those whom Aphrodite had chosen to regale.

Having now to prepare his own coffee, he sat at table, struggling to decide what music he ought to attend during the brief interval between this half-hour and those others soon to follow hard upon. He would have preferred to stay in bed. In truth, he would have preferred to be dead, dead and buried with his beloved next to him in a fitted box. Such was the disposition of the best and gloomiest student that was ever my pleasure.

The coffee was bad, but he forced it down anyway. These days he was living mostly on toast and jelly together with an occasional visit to a nearby eatery—"The Pied Cow" it was called—habituated by some of the most suspicious people the town had produced. As to what they were suspicious *of*, they never said.

Entering by the back door, he trudged to a corner table, making himself as insouciant-looking as he could. He had a cigarette dangling from the proper place, and in his left hand a volume on the Hindu gods with colored portraits. Fifteen clientele filled the narrow space, pure trash, most of them, though he had more lief stand in the front lines with one of these than amongst the insured businessmen three doors down.

Stationed in his place, he sometimes caught sight of faces worth looking at. He saw one now! A pudgy fellow with a bent nose, extinct eyes, each fist as big as two. They nodded each to each. What sort of awful activities had this person not carried out during his forty to fifty-five years on Earth? It didn't bear thinking of. It was just then that my student recognized that he had been carrying a paper of some kind in the breast pocket of his used jacket, a newspaper perhaps, or forgotten magazine that wasn't very thick, a brochure (probably political), or lecture notes left over from college days. Christmas cards or wrapping paper, he wasn't sure.

It was, in fact, a letter. He paid attention to the handwriting, an unusual script that might have been expected. A collection of twenty dollar bills fell out on the table, payment for "services rendered," she said. He scooped them up quickly and hid them away in the breast pocket of his previously-used jacket. He had no shame in accepting it. What was hers was his, and his would have been hers if only he had anything. The letter itself was lyrical in part and in other part quite pornographic, actually. I wasn't offered to read it, of course. Not that I would have refused. Research is research.

He now had the resources to buy another cup of coffee and did so. All his life he had planned to live a cultured existence without recourse to employment, a long-standing desire now seemingly within reach. He had gone far, had picked up all sorts of knowledge that would have slipped from memory without him. And as a corollary of that, a mere detail, he had added the world's most sumptuous woman to his résumé.

By contrast, his rooftop garden had gone to seed. Finally, in early November, he submitted to the advice of his alcoholic neighbor, a good man who had loaned money to him. Together they mounted to the roof, and in place of the ruined vegetables and sunflowers, plant-

ed two gross of bright green and yellow tulips made of
a plastic of some kind. Requiring neither rain nor attention, they offered a startling view to passers-by who
once or twice came to the door to talk about it. Two
weeks later, he was offered a price for the place, one
that would have discharged his debts while giving him
almost seven thousand dollars in capital gains.

Thursday, he hired himself to a well-heeled couple
in the valley who desired to clear a two-acre plot that
adjoined their home. A sorry pair, they had gained a
great deal by swapping their lives for money. They
would stand authoritatively at the edge of their yard to
be certain they were getting value for money. How odd
all things are! He could have thrashed both of them to
death with one hand only and had more information in
his fingernails than was dreamt of in their hollow
heads.

Came the weekend, he traveled to the town of Chal-
is, or rather tried so to do because the car broke down
before he was halfway there. He did, however, have a
good collection of tools in the car, and after about an
hour was able to have the thing moving again. Tonight's performance was to be of French music only,
and he arrived in good time to witness his favorite cellist, an iridescent woman in a blue gown that couldn't
have weighed more than five ounces. Six at most. Her
solo was good, of course, *very* good, but he had moved
beyond mere music by now. It was her face and the
way it combined with the rest of her, a unity that put
the audience, or half of it anyway, into a state of paraly-
sis. The more they wanted her and the more they
couldn't have her, the happier he was.

They looked at each other across the space, the
movement of her bow intended obviously for him. She
never closed her eyes at such moments—he didn't al-

low it. They were having trouble breathing. Thirty feet apart, they could nevertheless engage with each other in the lewdest fashion I'd ever seen.

He helped her with the case and instrument, rushed her to the car, and in order to safeguard her gorgeous blue gown, he removed that item and put it away safely in the glove compartment where it fit well enough when forced to do so. He was desperate. There was no doubt but that some of the passersby could suspect what they were doing. Both were crying, an arduous event punctuated by a muffled subtext of cries and screams.

They drove about the town. The Moon, though large, was sullied by a vapor that obscured it from normal viewing. Even so, the boy deemed it the best real estate anywhere.

"Okay," he said, "you can have the Sun. Me, I'll take the Moon. Especially when it's all covered up in vapor like that."

"Just a cloud, actually."

"Always the realist!"

He seized her, drove his tongue into her, and working counter-clockwise, tried to unscrew her right breast.

"Does that hurt?" he respectfully inquired.

"Isn't that what you want?"

"Me, I hurt all the time."

"I know, I know. Poor baby."

"Make it go away."

"I can't."

"Kill yourself."

"No, I'm too beautiful. Later, maybe."

He drove home slowly, covering nearly fifteen miles before returning to find the girl in one of his favorite callisthenic positions. She was wearing only a few items, and after a brief struggle, they were able to set her free. Cruel girl was she, and very soon she managed to put herself on top of *he*.

On his next attempt, he drove all the way home before arriving there. He had been listening to some really fine music that caused the girl's face to materialize in front of him, obscuring his view of the oncoming traffic. He was crying, of course, but had done such a great deal of that in recent months as no longer even to bring handkerchiefs with him, far less any of those little tearaway paper towels of about one square foot each.

He arrived home at half past three and immediately took to bed till the hour ended. He had to return to the car to shut off the music and retrieve his revolver. Someone had trespassed into the driver's seat, but hadn't been able to start the car. Back in his apartment, the boy tried to force down a dram or two of cough medicine and buttermilk, and then again went outdoors to check on the fragile Moon, characteristic behavior of his in the aftermath of the girl.

Came Tuesday, he was on the roof when two suited persons, one of them tall and the other not, called up to him from the sundial down below. He descended reluctantly but wasn't encouraged to shake with either of them.

"The Boy?"

"Yes, sir?"

"We have a matter to discuss with you. We could go inside if you prefer."

"Certainly. I still haven't done the dishes, however."

"Oh, that's alright. Okay with you, Charley?"

They all went inside. A new edition of *Pelléas et Mélisande* was on the machine, a fine performance that seemed to annoy the visitors.

"Could I offer you a cup of coffee?"

"Naw, I don't want any. You, Charley?"

"Naw. Beer, maybe."

He was a short fellow, Charley, and had some sort of civic decoration affixed to his lapel. Apart from this he had nothing more to say during the remainder of the session.

"We have some good news for you, Mr. ---------," the tall one said. "*Real* good. We're taking over this place of yours. The house and whatnot." He waved around at the property. "The whole kit and caboodle!"

"All of it?"

"And the flowers, too. What we have here, Mr. K--------- is a *new age* coming into focus, and we all have to adjust to it, you understand. You, me, everyone."

"I see."

"But here's the good part: *you will be paid*. Paid and paid well!"

"Good. But I think I'll just stay here."

They laughed.

Fifty-two

It developed that the county had need of a new eighty-bed facility, and with the help of the Cobbs organization, a 5.25 percent utility bond had been issued. Seventeen acres were required for the project, and whether the owners wished to sell or not had very little relevance when compared to the law.

Again, how strange things were. He had just this moment "made" a great deal of money without any effort of his own, a magical procedure that had done so much for the country. Far better was it to *deal* than to *do*—he would have to remember that.

The community did put forth an effort to save their homes and was even given twenty minutes in front of a judge of some sort, a grave individual, about sixty years old with a youthful wife.

In the event, it needed the boy just a single day to find new quarters, a one-room complex with toilet facilities further down the hall. He bargained with the owner, a youthful wife of a sixty-year-old husband who disliked the boy at first sight. No effort could convince the woman either to allow flowers on the roof or to alleviate the rent in return for certain custodial duties. She was hard.

At this date, the boy possessed about fourteen hundred pounds of personal property, most of it in books and iron tools. He imagined at first that he ought be able to transport those materials through his own efforts alone. With an ego like his, nothing could have given him more pleasure, never mind that his automobile was growing weaker by the day. He had a famous dictionary that alone weighed six pounds. Finally, toward nightfall, in exchange for his bedstead, he contracted with an antiques dealer to move the furniture in that person's covered van. The mattress he saved for himself.

He rested six days, until finally, on the following Wednesday, he jumped into his best clothes and strode toward town. They were not terribly good, his best clothes, but from a distance they gave off a certain respectability much at odds with a closer view. His socks were in deleterious condition, but his cufflinks had real silver in them and looked to be new. Dressed so, with two books under his arm and his revolver taped in place, he paced to the lawyer's office, and after signing a plethora of papers with two witnesses hanging over him, was given a check on grey paper worth precisely twenty thousand ninety-six dollars as itemized hereunder in rounded numbers:

Moving Expenses Allowed—$700 (giving him a

profit)
Prepaid Property Tax Rebate — $204
Refund of Environmental Impact Inspection charge
— $804
Reimbursement for 18 tropical fish with offspring
and spawn — $70
Dwelling — $4,250
Sundial — $18
Disused water well — $12
Land, 1.166 acres — $14,038

$20,096

He took the money and ran to the bank, but then had
to wait around while the teller verified the information.
He watched scrupulously as she counted out the money, one bill after another of mint-new currency bearing
the portraits of Northern generals on them. Thrilled beyond measure, he tried to tip the woman who at first
declined to take it. His next job was to alert his girlfriend, a good-looking music student introduced previously in this account. Communicating quietly by telephone, they added up their assets. The girl:

Savings from unexpended scholarship monies —
$3,821
Earnings saved from private cello lessons — $884
Harp lessons — $34
From sale of hand-painted dinnerware — $600–$700
(receivable)
Resale of diamond bracelet and other unsolicited
gifts — $1,668
Commission on the sale of parents' soybean harvest
— $2,085
Modeling fees — $8,823

$17,915

It came therefore to about thirty-eight thousand dollars for their joint wealth, a tremendous endowment that in truth was to give them the most they were ever to possess. They gloated over the telephone.

"You deserve it."

"What? No, *you* deserve it! You deserve it sixteen times more than I do!"

"Oh! Just because I'm beautiful? You had to work for it."

"Yeah. I work about two hours a day."

"And all those books you've read."

"They don't care about that! They don't even like it."

"Maybe we ought to do something."

"I'll be there Friday."

"No, something else. Maybe we ought to take a vacation."

He thought about it. "The sea?"

Fifty-three

But first he had to furbish his single-room apartment and make it more suitable for an occupant of his type. He scrubbed the floor, moved his books, and found a place for his iron tools. The mattress itself he located in the southeast corner furthest from the Sun. He had a radio, two matching socks, and a used refrigerator acquired for an unimaginably small price. And then, too, there were those objects he sometimes found lying at hazard in the alleyway that led to town. All his life, or at least since he had turned twenty-two, he had wanted to live off society's leavings, contributing as little as possible to the world while consuming even less. A fair bargain! He lived for himself.

Unwilling to invest his money in a system he de-
plored, he divided his cash into portions. The largest
share he stored in an otherwise empty pickle jar in the
freezer compartment of his antique refrigerator. Some
he put in Volume Three of Hodgkin's *Italy*, but then
took it out again just in the nick of time before returning
the book to the library. Some he put in other places, and
some in places even other than that. These days his wallet held more than ever, and with his good clothes and
his countenance the way it was, he could walk into any
store or restaurant he wanted and fool the world.

How he loved it! He who could have made a decent
living with minimum effort. He was young, smart as a
cat, not unhandsome, and yet had turned away from
what most people crave most of all. He could indict the
world without the world even knowing of it. Nothing
(except for one thing only) gave him greater pleasure.

"I see!" said I. "And so you can rub their faces in it
without anyone getting hurt!"

He grinned. "Humans believe they are important because they're human. I suppose grasshoppers feel the
same way about their own crowd. People have to have
a good opinion of each other to wish to hurt one another, right? Or have influence."

It was only my fourth interview with this exasperating personage, a two-hour meeting during which he
unfolded still another theory about the decay of civiliza-
tions. He was nervous and must have used up a dozen
cigarettes during the time. He had somehow come into
possession of a velvet jacket that didn't sort altogether
well with his trousers or the condition of his shoes.

"How goes the German?"

He seemed loath to talk about that.

"Good," he said. "Except for those goddamn prefixes
all the time. You start out thinking you know what

they're talking about, only to find out that you were wrong."

"Or maybe *they're* wrong."

"I'm going to wait till I get over there."

"Thought you were going to India!

"Later."

That was Monday. Two days later the girl herself came in, only the second time I had set eyes on this particular phenomenon. We had been recommended to each other by the boy, who had often spoken to her of my wide-ranging knowledge and other virtues.

She sat without moving. Her forest-green dress was conservative, and her wristwatch as tiny as a dime. She was proud, no question about that, and her face was both calm and melancholy to a degree. She was intelligent, a woman like Abelard's, and once again I began to experience the experience I had so inappropriately experienced before.

"Glad you could come," said I. "Coffee?"

I made it for her and stirred it with a curious little spoon acquired in Peru. She paid no attention to it, however.

"I wanted to thank you for coming to the concert," she said. "You had to travel so far."

"I go to all of them."

"Oh."

"The music was good, too."

The comment didn't please her.

"Next week he's going to . . ." (She mentioned a location on the Florida coast.) "He sold that old house, and he needs a vacation. He works so hard."

"I doubt it."

"He's so wild about the ocean. He has to look at it once in a while, he says. I think he should have been one of those explorers that used to find new places."

"He would have liked that, yes. But a person like that can find new places in all sorts of places. Even while sitting at a table. He's been my all-time favorite student, you realize, though I wouldn't give two pence for his future. Such a shame. Imagine, with just a little effort, he could almost have been like me!" I laughed loudly, laughing alone. "No, I wouldn't really want him to be like me."

"No."

"He is what he is."

"I think so, too."

"And that doesn't bother you?"

She was gazing out the window toward the smoke-infested mountains of eastern Tennessee, a far-away scene not available to older people.

"I never thought I'd actually meet him. I used to think it was too late."

"Too early or too late. That's the way things are, usually."

"I know."

"But you *did* meet him, right? Here, have some more of this good coffee."

We sat, gazing around at the books, smoke, mountains, the paperweight.

"But how can I let him go off to a place [Florida] like that and leave me here? It's not fair."

"Not in his condition, no. Say, maybe he should take you with him! It's worth considering."

"Yes."

"These things don't come along too often, you understand."

She looked steadily at me and at that moment gave up her secret, which forms the gravamen of my account.

"I'm ill."

"I hope not."
"Don't tell him."
"No."

Fifty-four

She didn't look ill, unless it were illness that had given her a loveliness as implausible as hers, a possibility mooted sometimes in classic books.

The day, too, was implausibly beautiful when the boy leapt aboard his worn-out car and, satisfied with its noises and other deficiencies, ran downstate to gather the woman. It still remained for her to prepare her lizards and put the last touches on her makeup. Together they studied her image in the mirror, the boy offering a few tiny suggestions that either she accepted or didn't.

"How does it feel?" he asked, "Being like you?"

She thought about it. "It's a big responsibility. But you get used to it."

"I'll never get used to you."

"That's sweet. But everything gets old after a while. I'm getting old while we sit here."

"Well, stop it."

"And then I'll just be a skeleton lying in the ground. Who will look at me then?"

His brain contracted suddenly, producing a fluid of some kind that sprayed the interior of his head.

"It can't be!"

"But it is. Look at me."

He focused on her in the mirror, a soul in golden foil, her perfect features and the far-away melancholy in her blue-grey eyes.

"I couldn't endure it."

"You'll have to. Or maybe," she said brightly, "it'll be the other way around."

"Hope so."

"And so you want *me* to do the suffering. Is that the way you are?"

They sat together quietly on the bench, clock ticking, automobiles passing in the street. If he held her close enough, perhaps she'd never go away.

They hit the highway in bright sunlight and ran off toward the Gulf of Mexico, four hundred miles away. Both people had contributed to the music hoard in the glove compartment, wonderful material, the best in all the world, nine-tenths of it from the Romantic Era. Her lips were red, and the impatient Sun had set her hair ablaze. Too much beauty, too much music, too much light, and too stunning an earthscape, with little red farms here and there. *This* surely was the time to die, just now, this very moment, the two of them transfixed with music, both of them poaching on the exact instant of youth's crescendo.

"Oh, God," she said.

Even more than when they were in each other's arms, this moment was sublime. He couldn't bear to look at her lest that face and figure, that sky-blue dress and luminous forehead, her prophet-bearing eyes, lest of an instant they turn to dust. He slowed, turned onto a farmer's road, and continued on until the way began to narrow. No one had been in this location for years, judging by the lapsing road and unharvested blackberries on all sides. Leaving the car, they walked up and down for a short time, awaiting the moment.

"Just think," he said, "life will never be like this again. Never, never, never."

"Oh, God."

"Everything is downhill from now on out."

They ran into each other's arms. She was so small, a thing of beauty, a mere wafer compared to the Sun; he lifted her to a level with his eyes.

"You're looking at me."

"I know."

"And I can see what you're thinking."

"What?"

"That you love me."

"Can't help it."

"What time is it?"

She delivered the time.

"Okay, write it down."

"Is this it?"

"Yes! For us, life will never be better than right . . . wait a minute . . . right now!"

"Oh, God!"

They flew into one another's arms and sank to the ground. Was this — yes — the most excelsior moment of their careers? Languid among the pines she lay, the Sun crackling in her hair. Was she even human?

They continued through a day that seemed to have been especially set aside for them as a one-time concession from the begrudging God. From certain indications, the flora and a lost gull, they believed they were approaching the coast. Still in the afterglow of life's best moment, their excitement took on new growth.

"Over there," he said, "that's where you'll first see the ocean."

"No, over there."

"Want to bet?"

A car passed by bearing a foreign license plate. It was large, the world, and they had time to sample every inch of it.

"Germany," he said, "that's where I want to go. Wagner was there."

"But ended up in Venice, I believe."

She was smart; he'd have to get used to that. The

Sun, mostly deplete by now and fighting for its life, was but inches from plunging into the all-begirding Ocean. The bats were out, mixed with gulls, while in the east a few precautionary clouds had put themselves into formation. He was looking forward to eleven o'clock, his favorite weather, when the salt-water waves would be contesting with the draw of the Moon.

"Getting closer!" he said, without looking at her.

"Can we go swimming tonight?"

"Of course."

"Good. I have a new bathing suit, and you won't be able to look at anything else."

And thus at some moment between six and seven in the very late afternoon, they came into a coastal city where ten thousand lamps, lanterns, and neon advertisements were ablaze in the crepuscule. It must have looked like Byzantium to them, young people more desperately in love than provided for by time and nature. He was sitting next to a wisp of beauty, more precious ounce for ounce than anything dreamt of in the periodic table. They halted in front of an office building where, in the window, the boy observed some half-dozen thralls working overtime at the close of day. Is this what life is for, and really, wouldn't those people prefer to be like him?

No one had ever been like him and never would, and never had anyone had a love like his and never could. He darted a look at the girl, who was looking right back. Now, now, now let life freeze in its tracks, while, as for future generations, let them come visit someday and see how happy boy and girl had been one time.

By their standards, the resort was a luxurious destination, and they were ready to squander up to four hundred dollars of their joint windfall. Striding importantly to the lobby, the boy began to question the woman at the desk. Apparently, the room was to have its own bathroom and other facilities. Meanwhile it was getting late, no doubt about that, and they had reached this place just in the nick of time. Soon, strange creatures would be emerging from the ocean, bad things capable of breaking down a person's door. Suddenly they ran together and, after kissing once or twice, handed off a tip to the man who stood waiting for it. He loved these types, did the usher, unmarried people who always gave too much.

"Ready to go swimming?" she asked, jumping like a child.

"I'd rather slice you open and eat your intestines."

"But can't we go swimming first?"

"Does that mean that you'll take off all your clothes while standing right there in front of me?"

"Do I have to?"

The usher seemed reluctant to leave.

"Certainly, you do! But let's have supper first, you want to?"

"But why can't we go swimming *now*?"

"Because there's still some people out there. When I'm with you, the ocean has to be for us only."

He went to a corner of the room and watched slowly as she got quickly into her skirt and hose. The skirt was cerulean blue, but the hosiery bothered him more. She had a brooch made of butterfly wings, a tourist item costing not much more than a loaf of bread.

The room was well-appointed, too, and contained a modern sculpture conveying a philosophic conception of some type. The curtains were yellow, and there were two brand new toothbrushes in an analogous number of plastic containers. Four towels, all quite fuzzy. The toothpaste itself was green, and both of them tasted of it. The girl was puzzled when the boy reverted to his customary loathing of such things:

"Did van Gogh need green toothpaste?"

Leaving their luxurious compartment, they paced down to the dining room and to a table where she could be viewed from different approaches. Everyone desired her, but no one could have her save himself alone; it was important that they understood this. He had brought his revolver, but didn't expect to need it, not among this prosperous and semi-civilized crowd.

By good luck, the waiter was not quite as snotty as expected. He recommended a certain wine, and after deep consideration, the boy consented to it. In fact, he was given a mere smudge of the stuff while the girl received nothing. He could feel his gorge rising. The menu itself, printed in Old English, was as tall and narrow as a folded newspaper. It alluded to all sorts of dishes unknown to either of them. He pointed to the name of a cheese and artichoke salad, a good choice apparently, that sent the waiter hurrying off to fetch it. It gave the boy a minute to focus on the calm, erect, alert, intelligent, and always somewhat melancholy phenomenon sitting just across from him.

"I look at you and . . ."

"I know, I know."

"It's killing me is what it's doing! And you just keep making it worse!"

"I know. It's worse for me, too."

"You are *unbearable*."

"I know. And I'm going to have to pay for it, too."

"I pay for it every day!"

"I know. But it's what you wanted."

"No, what I really want is to . . . Oh, I don't know. *Conglomerate* with you. Like two amoebas."

Came the waiter. The salad comprised not just the

aforementioned, but avocado, too, and sticks of celery. He tried to recalculate the cost of this meal. The girl was more accustomed to such surroundings, courtesy of the half-dozen persons who had wanted to marry her. There were enough silver spoons and crystal goblets in the place to have salaried the Confederate Army for a month.

"This is a *vile* society," he concluded. "Vile, vile, vile."

"I know, I know. But name me a good one."

From nearby tables, half a dozen diners were staring at them. How had such a one as he ensnared such a one as she? He grinned at them. The food was good, of course, perhaps five percent better than a frankfurter (frankfurter with sauerkraut) available for seventy-five cents on the other side of the street. They dined, appalled by the sight of middle-aged people—he could have thrashed any three of them by himself alone—striving to dance to a short-handed orchestra composed of saxophones, mostly.

They left their table when came the time for that and then ventured out to the verandah with its ocean view. The night was certainly a good one, as such things go, and the Moon was shining greenly over a sea much like the one that lay over against Cornwall in Tristan's day. Far from shore they saw a ship with lights aglow in the Captain's quarters, enough pirated spoons and goblets in that cabin, he supposed, to pay King Richard's ransom three times over.

"Should we go swimming now?" she asked.

"Far too late," he said, watching to see if she might cry.

Returning to their upholstered apartment, he ignited a cigarette and checked the lock, startled to find that the girl had somehow gotten into her one-piece white bathing suit before he could supervise the process.

"Dagnab it!"

"I know, I know. Next time. If you're good."

The sea was dark and green and had been set aside particularly for them. Oh yes, there might be a few fisherman still functioning on the wrong side of the world. They swam out a distance and then turned and critiqued the lantern-lit shore where hundreds of people had come together to wait out the night. The surf shimmied about their knees. Now and then a minnow bumped blindly into one or another of them before dashing off apologetically. Everyone knows about the Moon. Reflected in the standard ripples and routine waves, the light splintered into uncountable elements. Not so far away a dolphin emerged, ejecting gallons of sputum that lingered in the air. Sometimes a single moment stands in lieu of an entire epoch almost.

They embraced, providing the sight of two human figures stumbling clumsily against the grain of the current. Her face, luminous, joyous, dotted with ocean drops, drove him insane.

"It hurts me just to look at you. Hurts *bad*. I want to die."

"Not yet."

"When?"

Possibly she answered, though he couldn't hear her at just that moment in the surf.

They ran up and down the shore, the farm girl screaming each time he came close. Once before he had forced screams from her like those. He said:

"We've had two-and-a-half thousand years of Western civilization, and here are we, you and me, standing right smack in the middle of it. That's why it all got started in the first place."

"For you and me?"

"Precisely. But now Time is getting old and wants to rest."

"Not yet."

"When?"

Again, no answer came back to him from the ambient noises.

They swam a distance, but never so far as to let the sharks get at them. Knowing about the deleterious effects of salt water on numinous flesh, he soon extracted the girl and set her cello out of reach of the incoming tide.

"Play 'Claire de Lune,'" he required.

There were simply too many stars, too lovely a girl, too many phosphorescent things riding shoreward on glass-colored waves—he was in bad shape. Too much beauty all too abruptly presented, he was, I say it again, in *very* bad shape. Together they climbed to the hotel, went inside their place, and locked the door. The curtain was opaque. She was moist, and her suit had conspired with the devil to make her . . . You know what I mean.

"If you were any good," she said, "you'd help me out of this bathing suit."

"I have a weak heart."

"And you'd kiss me in *all sorts of places*."

"You wouldn't allow it."

"Don't make me wait."

She spoke. Her words had wings.

Fifty-five

He didn't know if he got any sleep that night. Reporting to me later, he described how they passed the following day splashing about in the water and sleeping in the sand. The clouds, he said, had come to a halt under the Sun, lending a coppery glaze to her hair. He doesn't know how long they lay there, sometimes sleeping, sometimes forcing their eyebeams as deeply as they would go into one another's over-heated brains. No shame, not even when a mob of little white crabs stood watching from no great distance away.

Came evening, they packed up their cello and other scant belongings and set out toward the west. It was not much past midnight, not yet dark enough for the boy to do his best driving. They encountered other cars and other drivers, supernumeraries foiling his dream that the girl and he had at last become the only people on the world. Or that they might go everywhere and see all things, venture in and out of abandoned cities, keeping vigil by night from lofty rooftops. And all this while the girl would still be there, smiling back at him through music and cigarette smoke. Things like that don't survive for long; he knew it, she knew it, they knew it jointly.

"Look at that Moon!"

"Beware lest it look back at you."

"Is that one of your philosophers?"

They were listening just then to the fourth movement of Mahler's Eighth Symphony, a superlative recording by the Utah Orchestra. Outside, the wind-distraught trees were slapping one another about the head and shoulders, and in one notable case, actually thrashing its arms against the ground. The car itself was old and thin, and a good-enough gust might shove them off the road entirely.

"Careful!" she recommended.

"Naw, they wouldn't dare."

An egoist on principle, he said: "You must never think of us as ordinary people, dear. Because we aren't."

But by one a.m. the Moon had disappeared, and the

advertisements that decorated the highway had lost some of their aesthetic value. They came to a traffic signal standing out in the middle of nowhere, a reminder that death might be waiting up ahead. He sped past a location where three roads came together.

"There," he said. "It was a place just like that where Oedipus killed his father."

"Good grief. Why?"

"And that windmill? Straight out of Bruegel."

"There?"

"No, no, that's just a gallows with a skeleton hanging from it."

"It's a tree!"

"Sure, that's what they want you to think."

"It is what I think. Want me to put on some music now?"

"Normally, yes. But not tonight."

They sped around a curve at thirty-six miles the hour, but then slowed as a concession to their ageing car. They passed an old-style Negro, his favorite kind, hobbling down the highway with a cane and a mess of catfish on a string. He witnessed, did my student, one of the larger stars blaze up suddenly and then fade out forever. How strange all things are! All those heavenly bodies and so forth, apparently they had come into being for the delight of those capable of being delighted by them.

"Did you see that star?"

She nodded.

"It's meant for us alone."

"Well, you did say one time that we're the only people in the world."

"Yes, I remember that."

"Except that nobody realizes it yet?"

"They'd be the last to know."

They came home just as the Sun was rising, leaving them with but moments to get inside.

Fifty-six

In the days that followed, they continued to pursue their lives from about thirty miles apart. He had wanted to go and take up in the same town, the same apartment indeed, but the girl wouldn't hear of it.

"No, we have to be new each time we meet. I'd rather die than let you get tired of me."

"That could never happen."

"And I don't want us to know too much about each other. Then you'd see how awful I really am."

"I like the awful part, too."

"No."

Forced by circumstances to do so, they replaced the car in October with a retired Studebaker left unattended by an elderly widow who wouldn't use it. They paid too dear for it and then paid even more to have a radio and heater installed. The car was suffused with an odd fragrance redolent of an earlier epoch, a feature that sealed the purchase. He didn't haggle over the price.

With a lot of money still remaining in their account, he found that he was working less and reading more. He knew a number of people who had rather work than read, preferring to build up their estates for the happiness of people who were as likely as not to prove despicable. Instead of that, he began to explore the Hindu wisdom, and after giving up on German with its vocabulary, jumped (temporarily) into the Slavic tongues, which he also failed to master.

"You want to be absolutely certain that you never actually learn anything, is that how it is with you?"

"I get bored," he said. "A person like me."

"And hard subjects are more boring than easy ones?"

"They're all boring for a person like me. Once I get the gist of it."

He was not, however, bored with the girl, and after three months of heavy use, the Studebaker also began to fall apart.

"Why not move in with her?" I promoted.

"I want to!" he said twice.

"But she won't have it?"

"No."

"She wants to be fresh and strange each time you meet?"

"Yeah."

God, she was smart.

Worse than October and bringing higher winds, November now had the girl running up and down the state and even beyond it to give recitals and participate in a quartet that was beginning to make a name, sometimes attracting audiences large enough to defray the cost of travel. She received another marriage proposal that month and actually accepted a modeling contract with a local hairstyling salon. She accepted the occasional flowers and jewelry, but declined a two weeks' stay in the Bahamas. But best was the seventeenth, when she was delivered a pink envelope mailed from Europe. Naturally, it wasn't until after she had opened the envelope and in due course had taken out the contents that she read the actual letter itself.

The message, from Romania, did contain a number of understandable phrases in English. She was being asked, beseeched rather, to join The Viteazul Orchestra on a temporary basis at a salary characteristic of the nation in question. Together with modeling, it would give her the best income of her career and go a long way toward the support of the boy in his ongoing struggles with the economic system. She had studied Latin in high school and expected to fit easily into this one-time Roman colony, provided her boyfriend consented.

"Absolutely not!" He laughed. "What would I do in Romania?"

"You could stay here."

"What did you say just now?"

"Stay here."

He laughed.

She needed permission from her college, and then would have to dip into their account for airfare. She spent two days at the farm, valuable time during which she saw to the mowing, and after some wrangling, managed to persuade the trombonist to look after the livestock and her father. She had to quit the quartet of course, which shortly afterward dissolved. It left her with just twenty-eight hours for the boy.

He yowled.

"No, no, no, no, no," and so on.

"I have to."

"You do *not* have to. You have to stay here. Staying here is the *exact opposite* of going to Romania. You want to join up with the gypsies? Well, go ahead and do so! What do I care!"

"It won't be long."

"Won't be long, she says. And what am *I* supposed to do? Sit around reading pornographic magazines?"

"No! I want you to stay away from those things!"

"It'll kill me. Might as well just kill me right here and now!" (He took up his three-inch Buck Knife, opened and locked it, and handed it to the girl.) "Here, just stick it in right . . . here!" (He showed where to stick it.) "Go ahead, I don't care. *You* don't care, *I* don't care. Go ahead! Get it over with! Nobody cares!"

I have no doubt he was crying again.

They had just twenty-three hours left to them.

Fifty-seven

He began by escorting her outside to catch the failing Sun in her hair. Time and genetics demand that boy loves girl, even if time and genetics sometimes go too far.

"Oh, God."

"I know, I know. It hurts me more than you."

"Very funny. Me, I'll be *dead* by the time you get back!"

"I'll hurry."

"Sure. And meantime you'll be loitering over there in that awful goddamn time zone with those people. Not even *I* can learn Hungarian."

"Romanian."

"Screwed-up verb system. And you think Japanese is bad?"

She laughed. It shouldn't be, beauty like this drawing him ever so slowly into the face of the scorching Sun.

"Not afraid of you," he claimed.

"Should be."

"I can't endure it."

"You must."

"I just can't!"

"Actually, you don't love me one-tenth as much as you should. If you did, you'd turn yourself into a tiny little mite and live in my ear."

"And go where you go?"

"Of course. Or until I get tired of you."

"You're already tired of me."

"Little bit."

He chased her to the next yard and forced her to the ground. The woman next door, the one on the porch with the broom in her hands, was not at all sure they were playing. Boy and girl were both crying by now, an established tradition between these two. She watched, the housekeeper, as with rough fingers he forced open the girl's mouth and tried to insert his head inside.

"I'm going to kill you," he revealed calmly.

"I want you to."

"And cut off your fucking head and eat it."

"Do it."

"I don't have any peace anymore!"

"You're not supposed to. That's why they sent me here."

"They?"

"Sure. Nobody can be as conceited as you and get away with it."

She smiled wickedly, edging him up to insanity once again. Would only they could sink about a hundred feet deep into that lady's backyard and repose together there for, say, about ten thousand hundred years.

In the event, they remained in the apartment till Tuesday, striving with but partial success to allay themselves with frenzied behavior. He kissed her feet. She tore his hair, and so on. But the earth in that district was so hard and cold, they weren't able to dig that above-mentioned hole in which to retire for all those years. He beat her. They wept. They dwelled in paradise.

Came Tuesday he drove her down to Atlanta, a well-attested location where in old times two surveying lines had intersected. They hated it. Both these people were accustomed to streets terminating in trees and green fields.

"I could read a book in the time it's taking that goddamn traffic light to change! Come here, people, come and take a look at the corpse! Here lies someone who used to be a man!"

"Oh, for goodness' sakes. I'm coming back!"

"No, you aren't. You'll be married to half a dozen people before that happens!"

They went on, passing successfully through a succession of traffic signs that seemed to contradict each another. He spotted an advertisement for a certain shaving cream and then a larger and even more artistic sign promoting a form of dental insurance.

"Is this what life is for?" he asked militantly. "The Greeks would have been nauseated."

"We can talk about it later, alright? I'm going to be leaving in just a few minutes."

She was right. Overhead, airplanes were coming and going at the rate of about one every two minutes, enormous vehicles threatening to land. At length he found a parking deck within walking distance of the airport, and after lifting out the cello and the heavier of the girl's two suitcases, set out on the first installment of the girl's long trip to Europe. He hated to see it, his gorgeous friend exposed to the curiosity of this country and that one, and their kind of people.

"Like to *kill* you," he said, speaking more loudly than he should.

"Ssssh! Later."

They pushed through the crowd, arriving in good time at an enormous city building the color of vomit. Together with the cello, they looked like *three* persons ascending the elevator instead of just the two we know them in fact to actually have been. The place held many foreigners, along with Americans of both the best and worst sorts. He spotted a seated woman reading avidly in a book that, upon closer inspection, seriously disappointed him.

"You'll have forgotten all about me before I even get on the plane!" the girl emitted suddenly. "It's always the same, people like you. I know."

He seized her, kissed her on the nose, and licked up both tears. Her face was gorgeous, and this was likely the very instant her beauty and character achieved its ultimate summit, as Spengler had said of certain cultures, furthermost utmost summit of her career. She had perhaps already begun to deteriorate even as he squeezed her.

"You won't be here when I get back," she said. "I realize that now."

He led her off, set the instrument aside, and kissed her rabidly on her reddening eyes. She was the prize of this world, his life's reason, nor had she even begun to deteriorate in any perceptible way. There was only one solution for the way he felt, but they were far from the apartment, and even that cure had never fully betided them for more than an hour or two.

"Oh, God."

"I know, I know."

"I can't stand it!"

"You? I'm the one that can't stand it."

"And I'll be here when you get back."

"Me? *You're* the one that's leaving, for Christ's sakes!"

"I have to."

"For your goddamn little career? Wish I'd never heard of it!"

"Then you never would of heard of me."

They ran into each other's arms. The passersby pretended to ignore them, save for an elderly man who had seated himself in order to watch. Had ever he (the old one) participated in an affair like this one? Not likely. And now, soon, the plane would be leaving, carrying her off to Europe and beyond.

He was to remember the moment she turned to look back at him, eyes full of tears, the waning Sun igniting her golden hair.

Imagine he had known then that he really wouldn't ever see her again.

Fifty-eight

He retired to their apartment and took to bed. Perhaps if he lay there long enough, she'd have returned by the time he grew conscious again.

He grew conscious again, but she was not there. He went through her belongings, finding not just the books and underwear he expected, but other materials related to an above-average interest in sexual matters. Knocked off balance by the stuff, some of it, he revved up her expensive machine and put on the Sibelius violin concerto, followed right away by the final three movements of Mahler's Eighth. He had pretty much given up on eighteenth-century music and intended to spend the rest of his life becoming more and more romantic, more so even than at present.

It was his intention to plunge back into his work, including especially his travails in the state archives. Keeping a noncommittal face, he sat directly across from the proctor, delving deeper and deeper into the private papers of certain figures who couldn't possibly have wanted such stuff made available. "Am I the only young person of my age in Tennessee who spends his time this way?" he asked, receiving no reply.

The girl would be over Europe by now, her adorable eyes sheltering under two fringed lids. Coming nearer, he sought to find the irises behind those thin membranes. Yes, she was sleeping, her mind having parlayed itself into a blue-green pond with lilies in it. Below, the map of lovely France was passing in review, a Valois territory replete with castles and flower gardens and the like.

He left the apartment, strolled two blocks, and lit up a cigarette. A movie show theater just then appeared up ahead where three roads ran together; taking two dollars and fifty cents of their joint money, he paid the fare and tried successfully to smuggle his burning book and cigarette into the building. Book, he meant to say, and slowly-burning cigarette. The film promised to be a good one, and by hap he had come in upon the face of a beautiful woman on the verge of a kiss. Not that she bore comparison to his own sweetheart, of course, whose eyes, so to speak, were a crime both against nature and all those timid boys frightened away by them.

The following scene was of little interest, but the one after that revealed the woman in a bathing suit. Her physique was of the American type, nice enough, he admitted, but lacking the sort of *décolletage* he required in the better sort of ladies' beachwear. Sadly, he was just two seats away from a crowd of people of approximately his own age, imbeciles making comments anent the sound of chewing. He wanted to rise and move away, and would have done so but for his tumescence. The movie star was bending over to gather up her towel.

Sick by natural inclination, he could never be calm again, not till his sweetheart had come back to him. He was nervous, too, and his cigarette had worn itself out without any effort of his. But mostly it was the actress' face that upset him; better these people were bees or ants and all looked just alike.

He walked home in a light drizzle that partly calmed him and let him look forward to the reading he had planned for that night. Owing to events, he had begun to look into the mysteries of Romanian history, especially that thousand-year period during which either nothing had happened or else no one had written it down.

Of course, he could always fill in the blanks with imagination.

Fifty-nine

She had arrived in Bucharest at just after nine and
gone direct to her hotel. She disliked it when the taxi
driver went on staring at her in the mirror, and although she had memorized perhaps fifty words of the
language, it wasn't enough to detach his gaze. Her skirt
of course was short, an adjunct to her philosophy, and
in any case she had already stretched it out as far as
possible. If her legs were beautiful, were it not a cruelty
to keep them hidden? She had a duty to reify herself.
And, then, too — why not admit it? — it gave her a thrill.
She couldn't know her boyfriend was suffering at just
that moment in a downtown movie theater.

She dined (delicately) in the hotel restaurant, an ex-
quisitely-appointed place with high-priced foods. She
could have bought my student a pair of new shoes on
the cost of an aperitif. She experienced some guilt that
the charge was to an impoverished orchestra in one of
Europe's most questionable places. In the event, she
had a pro forma salad, white wine, and nothing else.

Her room was aesthetically-appointed, too, and held
a spare toilet (bidet) that mystified her. She tried the
television, but found the spoken language far too rapid.
Finally, she spread the blanket on the floor and went
quickly through a series of exercises that you and I
could not likely have replicated. The radio gave good
music while concentrating just a bit too much, she felt,
on a certain composer who happened to have been a
native of the place. She showered, first placing a chair
to reinforce the door. The mirror was old and out of focus from too much usage.

She gave no more than forty minutes to the cello and

then jumped in bed and mounted the pillow. Whence comes the notion that a person oughtn't do things like that, look in a mirror and use a pillow? It wasn't of course the same as actually being penetrated by a certain one, but in the meantime would have to do. And sometimes she wished (not really) that she were still an innocent girl for whom the birds used to come and sing.

Came morning, she hit the street in bright Sun and sallied off on a three-hour tour of the famous city. There are places where a woman will draw quite enough attention by dressing conservatively with head held high. It isn't true that women are dominated by men, not when a woman walks in the optimum way. She strolled slowly, testing the temper of this essential city, and then took a taxi to the concert hall, where soon she would have to earn her pay. By late evening she was back in her hotel, a musty place of antique furniture, massy portraits on the wall, and thick red drapes endued with nineteenth-century dust—she adored it.

The restaurant occupied one whole floor of the building and was perpetually attended by a definite number of odd-looking people. A tiny orchestra was lodged in the corner, and although the evening was early, the players were tired and old already. Someday, as her gloomy boyfriend liked to say, the whole world would be like this. She perceived the cellist, an elderly woman with too much lipstick and a goiter. There was undoubtedly some good music to be had in this city, but as for the people themselves . . . She had been warned.

She exercised at length, too much really, and then took out and studied the cello score she would be required to play later on. She had been apart from her man and her lizards for more than thirty-six hours by now, and yearned grievously, if not equally, for all of them.

The bed was enormous and had been used, she felt sure, by cellists and cardinals, yea, King Carol himself, mayhap. She bathed and freshened and depilated herself in the pattern demanded by her man. He had no dislike of her luminous hair, certainly! She used no deodorants, of course, another of his requirements. She tried not to think of him, however, and shortly after eleven o'clock, managed to fall off to sleep.

When according to wont the Sun, her own special star, arose from regions more easterly than Bucharest, she leapt from bed and did her exercises. Always aware of "time's chariot" drawing near, she deemed herself about as pretty as she had ever been, not to mention more sophisticated by a great deal. Having a glass of wine at a table of her own in ancient Bucharest with men staring at her (she did not feel naked when men stared at her, but only when they didn't), she could go in safety whithersoever she wist.

It was at this table that she inscribed her third and fourth letters to the reprobate back home in Tennessee. No one seeing her at that time and noting her worthy silhouette, her far-away melancholy and immaculate tailoring, no one, I say, could have imagined the sort of material those letters contained. I've seen them.

She returned to her room, adjusted herself, checked the mirror, and then hefted up the cello—the wench was strong—and carted the thing out into the fraught purlieu of easternmost Europe. The people she saw! And yet others appeared fully evolved, assets to Western civilization as she supposed. A man hurried up to help with the cello while two others followed at a distance. I could have told them their chances.

She strolled past all sorts of shops calculated with devilish insight to appeal to a woman's cockles. Small things, very cute, even adorable indeed. But she dasn't use up any of their joint money, the boy's and hers. An adolescent, an awful one, now came up and offered his assistance, as she interpreted it. Instead, she turned into Strada Demetru Dobrescu and slithered into a crowd of reasonable-looking people of middle-age or better. The women, some, were more tastefully dressed than they needed to be; she could feel her gorge rising. She spotted a more or less handsome man who, however, wouldn't have lasted five minutes against her boyfriend. She was strong (see above), but was beginning to tire after having trekked the six to eight hundred yards to the building assigned to her.

She had the stamina to carry her fiddle up three stories and into the office of the man to whom she was obliged to report, a portly individual who right away began welcoming her in the uncanny language of the region. She had studied a bit of Latin, but this was foreign to her. He looked her up and especially down and then called an English speaker from the adjoining office who focused instead on her lapidary face.

"Well!" he said. "Yes. And so you're here now."

She agreed.

"He wants to welcome you to Romania," he said, nodding to his superior. "He wants you to enjoy your stay here with us—this is what he's saying. And remember this—he doesn't understand a word of what we're saying. You can speak freely. But tell me, are you satisfied with your lodging arrangements?"

"Of course. I grew up on a farm."

"Really! You don't look like it."

"And plan to go back eventually."

"Truly? Nobody in this country wants to live on a farm. However, we *are* becoming a more tolerant place, I think. More equal. To say the truth, I'm not sure we really need any orchestras anymore."

The girl didn't comment.

"I don't suppose you've met the conductor yet? He's anxious to see you."

She was made to sign a few papers, none of which she could decipher, and then was given a laminated identification card bearing a two-year-old photograph that the organization had somehow acquired. The original man was still speaking, still smiling, still betraying his wife with every glance.

The conductor — she knew a little about him already — was as normal-looking as the original man wasn't. She noticed at once two aspects of his personality, namely that he spoke a form of English, and secondly that he didn't care a whit for how beautiful she was. She sat erect in Victorian dignity, a nineteenth-century cameo in a short skirt

"New person, yes? Cello?"

"Yes, sir."

"Not much experience."

"Some."

"Good, good. Good. Rehershal [sic] seven p.m. o'clock."

She left.

She wanted to inspect the concert hall in more detail and did so now, this time resorting to an unpainted taxi with a multicolored driver. The streets in some ways might almost have been found in America, but in other ways not. They tended to keep well away from each other, the cars and people, her own natural tendency as well. A drunk man was slumped against one of the storefronts; another was wearing a fez.

She paid the driver (too much) in American money, which he did not refuse. An old-style individual, he actually helped with the cello and spoke courteously, employing one or another of the languages there in use. It was a nuisance, taking her instrument everywhere she went, but did at least prevent it being stolen from her hotel room. The concert hall was appealing to her, a rococo pile that put her in a "European" mood, if you take my meaning. She thought that perhaps she should stay (stay in Europe) if these people really respected cellists as much as appeared.

She strode to the front door of the auditorium, collecting further respect from the janitor lunching out of a paper sack. He stood at once and pulled open the door for her—such is the regard for beauty in southeast Europe. There's much to be said for societies of that kind. She stood for a time appraising the stage from the point of view of an attendee in cheap seats. From this vantage, she ought to be entirely visible, she believed. How strange that she would herself be on stage in just one day and eleven hours from this present time.

Finding no taxicabs with trustworthy drivers, she walked two blocks in what she believed to be the correct direction before stopping all of a sudden and racing back for her cello. Arriving home, she saw that someone had entered her room, leaving the bed even better-made than she had left it. However, she was a little bit enfeebled by her long walk and the recurring effects of that lifelong disease that was to kill her before much longer, before she had "used up" her beauty, she liked to say. "A better thing than enduring old age." She rested, therefore, briefly, and then arose, showered, and exercised, or exercised and showered rather, and then took out the score and began studying it most sedulously.

Sixty

On the ninth day, he received three letters all at once. Postal service was bad in Europe, and the ink she used was by no means of the best quality; indeed, he had seen better in certain old nineteenth-century diaries stored in state archives. Had someone been reading over her shoulder? The letter was far too cool and even official, the language reflecting little of the passion that he expected in messages addressed to him. He fell into depression.

The second letter was better. She had touched down in east-central Europe and had gone off by herself to a telephone booth, where she could write openly about matters afflicting them. She wanted to come home. She had been crying. She ached for another dosage of what he alone knew how to supply. She hated it already, the place to which she was going. She enclosed two strands of golden hair, one of which he put away in his wallet and the other of which he consumed.

(The first "letter," in fact it had been nothing but a postcard legible to anyone who cared to look at it. Hence the few weak lines it had conveyed.)

The third and the last letter of the day detailed how she had been to the embassy to learn how to come home. He had to wait four more days to read that she had performed two times on stage and was waiting for him in a third-floor hotel room in central Bucharest. The embassy, a sympathetic group, had given her a stick of peppermint, a little brown teddy bear, and a ride back to her hotel.

Regarding his own letter to her, it was seven pages long owing to the poetry and drawings incorporated into the body of the text. Carrying it by hand to the Post Office, he paid the fee to Bucharest, knowing it would need weeks to arrive there. Would she still be beautiful then? More importantly, had anyone ever been as beautiful as he thought that he remembered her to have been? Nothing worried him more than that she might have turned into a standardized postmodern woman before he saw her again. Cheerful, ignorant, optimistic, and the rest. Vacuous as air, and so on. The sort that loved her children more than her man.

His next letter, inscribed late that evening, told how he had acquired four hundred tulip bulbs at a giveaway price and had planted them in the most artistic fashion around the gazebo of one of the nearby aristocrats. His employer, predisposed to treat inferior people in kindly fashion, had smiled maternally and given him a soft drink. Perhaps he might still measure up to higher standards someday.

He never worked longer than three hours a day. More than that, and he would be contributing more to society than society warranted.

"But don't you think," I asked him once, "that you should give back to the world as much as you take out?"

"Sure! That's why I don't take out very much."

He wrote the first part of the next letter the following morning, finishing it that night. That he was insane, he didn't try to hide it. Nor that in the fullness of time he hoped she might join him in that career. A woman in love will do anything whatsoever, provided the man be unwavering enough.

"Want me to go to hell for your sake? I will." This is the actual line which, having written, he had to wait three weeks to see if she'd reciprocate.

He traveled that weekend to her parents' farm and spent most of the day with the cattle and making a needed repair to the barn that every day seemed to be leaning more and more to one side than toward the others. He had no special liking for the cows, a bovine genotype consecrated solely to their own immediate interests and not much else. He did speak kindly to them, however, grateful for their passivity.

He was given a meal by his girlfriend's people, rural fare including the first cornbread he had tasted in years. They were proud of their two standard daughters, but only somewhat proud of the divinity who composes the main theme of this account.

"We sort of hoped she might find a job," the mother offered.

"Or get married."

"She was so good with the livestock, don't you know."

He endured it. They had some art on the parlor wall that resonated with him, particularly an equestrian scene of Nathan Forrest in full uniform. They had an old piano that had been used by no one apart from their extinct son, a full-scale imbecile who used to pound on it.

At this time, the nights were growing chill enough for the old man to open the grate and set up the first fire of the season, a coal-fueled affair that started off as a yellow thing before turning white as the flame grew hotter. He was given, the boy, a jar of cider which he consumed quickly and gladly, as did also the others. Each his own jar, of course. Turning silent as evening wore on, the group studied the two score of smoldering coals going through a series of tormented facial expressions.

He insisted on sleeping in his girlfriend's adolescent bedroom, a favor they were loath to grant. There were some clothing articles in there, together with the faint, far-away scent of the woman herself. He suffered. Proceeding with delicacy, he opened the six drawers, the first one first, and spilled their contents on the bed. The actual contents of those drawers, the closet, and the area beneath the bed were not disclosed to me.

He woke late, but then quickly went to work with the harvester, a used-up machine out of manufacture long before. Even so, he was good at mechanics, decently good, and after hurting himself with the wrench, he went to claim his meed of a cinnamon roll and two cups of sweetened coffee.

"Had a letter," the farmer said. "Seems like they got her playing in that band over there."

"Good! What else does she have to say?"

"Addressed to *me*, that letter."

"Oh."

"Got her living in a *hotel*. I suppose it's just as well we didn't go with her."

"And there're the animals," the boy reminded them.

"No, they *sure* wouldn't let us take them."

"No. Anyway, I think I've got your harvester up and running again."

"Don't have any harvesters."

"He's talking about that old thing that got left here."

Just then and for the second time that day, the rooster began ululating from the western gable, a hopeless effort to communicate all the way to Bucharest.

Sixty-one

On the eighteenth of December, she participated for the first time in a European orchestra of good quality. It wasn't the Berlin Philharmonic, to be sure, and the conductor wasn't Karajan, but it was better than hog chitterlings and black-eyed peas for a girl who wasn't twenty-two years old as yet. She had many friends (males) and many enemies (women) in that assemblage, albeit her friends proved too coy, most of them, to come within arm's length of the girl.

She played her part passably well, the conductor told her, not too hot and not too cold. She replied in her

fashion, telling the man that he had done passably well
as well. Would they, or not, ever allocate to her a solo to
display her musicality and appearance? A few minutes
on a golden harp? Publicity photographs, both in color
and black and white? Pictures to make her lover more
insane than he was already? An emissary from the
King? Of all those possibilities it was only the first one,
the one starting off with "would they," that she considered very likely.

She strolled the town, collecting bits and pieces of
that uncanny language from off advertising signs.
Dressed in a winter coat and head covering, the city
thralls no longer shouted at her. This hurt. She purchased a recording of a performance in which she had
participated and mailed it to the boy. If he loved her,
loving her truly, he would know which notes were hers.
She bought a silver blouse with metal buttons. This was
same day she had her first real episode when, at just
after eight p.m., she fell unconscious in her hotel room
and didn't come awake till three hours (!) later.

Nearly always, she dined in the hotel's own restaurant, ordering such slight meals as to have made herself
an object of exasperation and affection among the staff.
Tuesday, they offered her a sprig of watercress and
nothing else. To which on Wednesday she replied with
a box of chocolates costing about five American dollars.
In her lonely room, she still practiced assiduously, not
neglecting the pre-Romantic material she didn't really
much care for. There was no doubt but that Haydn had
been a fine man, however. She had a supply of extra
strings in case her rivals wished to sabotage her instrument. She invested in a gram of powdered eye shadow
of a type previously unknown to her, employing the
stuff on her first venture to one of the downtown res-
taurants. It was so strange—her apparel was entirely

respectable, almost conservative really, but the men who saw her were just as upset. Excited by this, she hastened back to her room to write her friend and tease him a little bit.

She was so young and was so much what she was, why couldn't it go on forever? Because then she'd get bored.

Tuesday came again the following week. She was more or less resigned by now to her situation when in mid-January she was permitted to open the *Heldenleben* of Richard Strauss. She loved those measures, dedicating them in her mind to her far-away manipulator. She wore a silver blouse with metal buttons, but no one complained.

Wednesday came next, a quiet time during which only the notes she made in her lonely room need be noted here.

After that, more than five weeks went past before the first of March at last came up all bright and clear. She had, during this time, shared in more foreign performances than at any earlier period in her American career. She had received another proposal along with a spate of letters inscribed in Romanian, sometimes Hungarian (if she guessed rightly), and one in Danish. I do not mention the messages from her stateside swain.

How she yearned for him! Her bed was narrow, but not too narrow to hold a boy. She had found another pillow in the closet. And this, that her yearning must go on forever, or anyway till she had turned back to atoms once again. And sometimes she yearned for that as well.

On the other hand, she *was* alone most of the time, and free to apply herself to herself as opposed to society and the outside world. Already she had read most of the books assigned her by her evil friend, and had even progressed far enough in written Romanian to toil her way through an elementary-grade children's book with pictures in it. Too lovely for a long life, she strove to fulfill her destiny — exercising, primping, dieting, referring now and again to the sexual literature that her mother had provided at the start of her affair. She brought herself up to date for next year's chemistry class, using an outline I myself had prepared. Concise, clearly written (I believe), the thing continues to be available at nominal cost, plus postage.

Sixty-two

Time to get ready for the end of things. She had been doing her stockings in the all-too-tiny sink and was hanging them up to dry when she grew dizzy of a sudden, staggered, and fell to the hard tile floor. I imagine her there. Don't know whether she lingered for a time or fled straightway to the non-existence awaiting her ever since she was offered inhuman beauty in return for her brief tenure on Earth. Don't know if she called out or not. Don't think it was in her character to do so.

She was found in the late afternoon, whereupon the management at once notified the government office, the conductor, her hometown music school, and her parents, in that order. Almost senile by this date, her father sat for a long time, looking down at the floor. "I guess you have to expect things like this," he told me later on. "It's a bad situation all around, when things happen. Seems like there's always something going on somewhere."

His wife, a more hysterical sort of person, ran outside and then ran back in, furious with music, the boy, Romania, and the girl herself.

I should stop here but for this last business — information I was able some seventeen months later to squeeze out of that country's horrid bureaucracy. Something from a friend of mine with a position in the State Department.

The girl waited three days to be cremated in assigned order, when suddenly an American of some sort had emerged from the elevator and, with the help of two hirelings and a large bribe (large by East European standards), had taken the corpse over into his own possession. That's all I know, sorry.

ABOUT THE AUTHOR

Tito Perdue was born in 1938 in Chile, the son of an electrical engineer from Alabama. The family returned to Alabama in 1941, where Tito graduated from the Indian Springs School, a private academy near Birmingham, in 1956. He then attended Antioch College in Ohio for a year, before being expelled for cohabitating with a female student, Judy Clark. In 1957, they were married, and remain so today. He graduated from the University of Texas in 1961, and spent some time working in New York City, an experience which garnered him his lifelong hatred of urban life. After holding positions at various university libraries, Tito has devoted himself fulltime to writing since 1983.

His first novel, 1991's *Lee*, received favorable reviews in *The New York Times*, *The Los Angeles Reader*, and *The New England Review of Books*. Since then, he has published eleven other novels — including *The New Austerities* (1994), *Opportunities in Alabama Agriculture* (1994), *The Sweet-Scented Manuscript* (2004), *Fields of Asphodel* (2007), *The Node* (2011), *Morning Crafts* (2013) *Reuben* (2014), and the *William's House* quartet (2016) — which have been praised in *Chronicles: A Magazine of American Culture*, *The Quarterly Review*, *The Occidental Observer*, and at *Counter-Currents*.

In 2015, he received the H. P. Lovecraft Prize for Literature.

www.ingramcontent.com/pod-product-compliance
Lightning Source LLC
Chambersburg PA
CBHW051257250626
47155CB00009B/3326